"I lied," Sam murmured

Slowly he reached out, his hands splayed against the back of Abby's thighs as he pulled her closer to his chair.

"Lied?" she whispered. Her lips were suddenly dry, but as she licked them with the tip of her tongue, she knew she'd made a tactical error. Sam's eyes flared with hunger.

"Lied. I told you I slept fine, but I didn't. I didn't get any sleep at all last night, Abby. I kept thinking of how it was going to be when we finally made love...."

JoAnn Ross's latest Temptation is a marvelous tale of intrigue, adventure and, of course, romance. This creative writer tells us Sam and Abby "came" to her one day, and she simply wove the story around them. JoAnn lives in Arizona with her husband and teenage son. Currently at work on a new Temptation, she's also been published under the pseudonym JoAnn Robb.

Books by JoAnn Ross

HARLEQUIN TEMPTATION

42–STORMY COURTSHIP
67–LOVE THY NEIGHBOR
77–DUSKFIRE
96–WITHOUT PRECEDENT

HARLEQUIN INTRIGUE

27–RISKY PLEASURE
36–BAIT AND SWITCH

These books may be available at your local bookseller.

Don't miss any of our special offers. Write to us at the following address for information on our newest releases.

Harlequin Reader Service
901 Fuhrmann Blvd., P.O. Box 1397, Buffalo, NY   14240
Canadian address: P.O. Box 2800, Postal Station A,
5170 Yonge St., Willowdale, Ont.   M2N 6J3

A Hero at Heart

JoAnn Ross

Harlequin Books

TORONTO • NEW YORK • LONDON
AMSTERDAM • PARIS • SYDNEY • HAMBURG
STOCKHOLM • ATHENS • TOKYO • MILAN

To Margaret Carney, whose contagious good humor
never fails to brighten my day. And to Birgit
Davis-Todd, whose marvelous eye for detail keeps
me honest.

Published July 1986

ISBN 0-373-25215-3

1

SAM GARRETT STOOD in the shadows, watching her. Silvery moondust streamed into the room, lighting everything with a mystical glow. The French doors were slightly ajar, allowing the sweet scent of roses from the garden to fill the air and mingle enticingly with the heady, Oriental cloud surrounding Jessica Thorne. Her skin gleamed a translucent pearl in the muted light as her lover's lips burned a path across her bare shoulders.

"God, you're beautiful," the man murmured, a fact with which Sam readily concurred as his calculating eyes followed the heated trails the man's palms made over her lush, womanly curves. "I can't believe my luck."

Jessica's full lips showed a smile of sheer feminine satisfaction as her fingers laced through the man's blond hair. "We're both lucky," she said in a breathless whisper that was part honey, part smoke.

Her distinctive voice was the result of a case of laryngitis in her teens that had left behind a deep, husky resonance. Even knowing that little detail didn't lessen its appeal, Sam decided, unable to explain his unprofessional feelings of fascination concerning this woman. Not only had he been thoroughly briefed, he'd been following her for the past two weeks, learning a myriad of little facts about her life.

But that in itself was not so unusual; he was never one to overlook those minute details that would eventually enable him to snare his quarry. What was out of the ordinary, however, was the way he'd become overly interested in everything about this woman. If he'd been forced to choose a word to describe these uncharacteristic feelings, he would have chosen *obsession*. But that smacked of weakness, and Sam Garrett was not a weak man.

Her slim fingers were toying with the buttons of his shirt, teasing the junior senator from Oregon unmercifully as she took her time freeing him from the barrier of material between them.

"Oh, Jessica," he groaned. "I never can get enough of you."

She laughed, a rich, musical sound, and her gray eyes sparkled like quicksilver, rivaling the shimmering moondust for brilliance.

"I thought you said we had all night," she murmured, shifting so she was lying across him on the king-size bed, her long hair splayed like strands of ebony silk over his body.

His hands ran up the back of her thighs. "We do. And believe me, sweetheart, we're going to make the most of it." With one deft movement he placed her under him.

As he viewed the erotic scene, Sam experienced a harsh, unwelcome feeling of possessiveness. *She's just a job*, he reminded himself silently, his gaze narrowing as the man pushed a strap of the scarlet slip off one shoulder, his lips brushing over her satiny skin.

Sam was not the only one watching the twosome. Lost in their lovemaking, neither Jessica nor James Kent had heard the woman enter through the French doors.

"Well, isn't this a cozy little scene."

For a moment, both parties froze, then James turned, his complexion a sickly, ashen shade. Jessica propped herself up onto her elbows, her eyes brightly alert as she prepared for Meredith Kent's fireworks.

The senator seemed less enthusiastic about the unexpected arrival of his wife. "Meredith! I didn't expect you back tonight."

The young woman's face was set in stone, her lips a firm, grim line. "I'd say that's obvious. Mother's much better."

"I'm glad to hear that," he answered weakly, the banality of the statement hanging heavily in the air.

"I'm sure she'll be pleased to hear how concerned you were. After all, you *are* her favorite son-in-law." Censorious green eyes moved to Jessica, who'd yet to enter into the conversation. "Doing a little nighttime lobbying, Mrs. Thorne?"

Jessica Thorne's poise did not falter. This wasn't the first time she'd been in this situation, and she knew it wouldn't be the last.

"One does what one can, Meredith," she said simply. "More work is done after hours than ever gets done between nine and five. You've lived in Washington long enough to know that."

Meredith Kent's eyes widened as she observed the other woman's unconcern. She reached into her purse, pulling out the small caliber revolver with remarkably steady hands.

"Meredith! For God's sake, put that down!" Her husband rose to his knees, reaching out for the gun, his hand shaking visibly.

"Don't move, James. Or I'll have to kill you, too," she warned him, not taking her eyes from the scantily clad woman in her bed.

"Meredith, darling, don't be such a middle-class bore," Jessica drawled.

"Meredith, I swear this is the first time . . ." James's voice dropped off as his wife cocked the hammer, using both hands to hold the gun steady.

The sulfurous smell of gunpowder igniting overcame the soft scent of roses as a shot rang out. Jessica slumped back onto the pillows, a dark stain spreading across the her crimson silk slip. James Kent screamed as his wife stood statue-still at the end of the bed, holding the smoking handgun at her side.

As Sam watched silently from the sidelines, his only reaction to the crime of passion was a slight flinch. His eyes remained riveted on the wounded woman's supine figure.

"Cut! All right, boys and girls, that's a wrap. Let's get the hell out of here and I'll see you all in three months."

"Yuck." Abby Swan rose from the bed, hating the stickiness of fake blood against her skin. Slipping into the robe provided by the costume mistress, she wanted only to escape to her dressing room.

"Will you be back, Abby?" The boyishly attractive director stepped in front of her, cutting off her planned escape.

Abby sighed. She'd been over this so many times she felt she should simply record her answer onto cassettes. Then, whenever anyone asked the question, she could just hand them a recorder and tell them to push Play.

"I really don't know. If I get the funding for my film, I'm not going to sign the new contract."

"And if you don't get it?"

She shrugged, giving him a crooked smile. "I'll probably be back. After all, I have to eat, right?"

In truth, Abby knew that no matter what happened with her beloved project, she didn't have to return next season due to any financial concerns. Her role as the amoral Jessica Thorne in television's smash nighttime soap opera, *Potomac*, had made her a wealthy woman. Then there was always her trusteeship at Swan Pharmaceuticals. But acting was her lifeblood. She couldn't simply sit around her house, waiting for the right part. She had to keep working, even if she was bone weary of being the woman America loved to hate.

She patted his cheek, attempting to move past him. "Have a good vacation, Lance."

"If you're holding out for more money," the man suggested, "you'd better quit being so intransigent. After all, you won't be the first star to be written out of a series. Jessica isn't immortal," he warned.

"None of us are," she agreed amiably.

"Why in hell do you want to go into production anyway? All the fame is in front of the cameras," he argued.

"I've had my share of fame, Lance. The way I see it, the only way I'm going to get more challenging roles is to produce the scripts myself."

Sam heard it before he saw it. A slight creaking noise, then a sharp crack. Instinctively, he raced toward the couple, hurling his large bulk against her. Abby cried out as she was thrown to the ground, her body smothered by the hard male frame. An instant later, a large light crashed to the floor, landing where she'd stood only a moment before.

Her planned protest dissolved in her throat as her eyes cut first to the light, then to the scaffolding overhead, finally meeting the intent amber gaze inches from her own.

"Are you all right?" Sam asked in a rough voice.

Abby shifted underneath him. "I think so. But I'll be able to tell a lot easier when you get off me."

"I'm sorry about that, but I didn't have any choice."

As the man stood, Abby stared up at the stranger towering over her. He was tall, well over six feet, she determined judiciously. His hair was cut a bit shorter than she preferred, but upon closer examination she decided he probably kept it closely clipped in order to control those crisp chestnut waves. He was far from handsome, but his harshly hewn face possessed a formidable strength that she found oddly compelling. He was looking down at her with cool amber eyes that appeared curiously remote considering he'd been sprawled over her nearly naked body only moments before. Most men couldn't resist a leer when meeting Jessica Thorne in person.

She was about to say something when Lance was suddenly jerking her to her feet. "Christ, Abby, you're a walking disaster zone these days. I've never seen anyone with a worse run of luck."

She stared mutely at the light that could have solved the question of Jessica once and for all. If she hadn't been thrown out of the way. . .

Abby shook her head, refusing to consider that idea. It had been another accident. That's all. Like the air gauges going haywire while she was scuba diving off the Baja coast. Or the fire that had gutted her kitchen in the predawn hours of the morning. Her smoke detector had awakened her in time to escape that little incident, although she'd been shaken to think that without that fifteen-dollar investment, her entire home could have gone up in flames, herself along with it.

Not liking Abby Swan's suddenly pale complexion, Sam took her by the arm, directing her forcefully over to the bed. "Sit down," he instructed. "You look like you're going to faint."

Although Abby was admittedly grateful for this stranger's prompt response to this latest accident, she wasn't wild about his proprietary manner. "I never faint," she protested as she sank down onto the mattress.

"Sure," he shot back, pushing her head down between her knees. "But there's always a first time, and right now you look like death warmed over. Stay that way," he ordered, turning back to the equally ashen director. "Who the hell is in charge of lighting around here?"

Lance Griffen was used to issuing orders on his sound-stage, not taking them. His shock turned to irritation but before he could come up with a caustic retort, a third man appeared on the set, his eyes sweeping over the scene. "Oh, my God," he groaned, "there goes my union card."

Sam spun around, fixing him with a cold stare. "Are you in charge of this stuff?"

The young gaffer, wearing a T-shirt and painter's pants, appeared honestly distraught. "That's me. And I swear, that light was bolted into place." He appeared prepared to argue his case, but Sam didn't press the point.

"I believe you," he said, turning abruptly back to Abby. "Let's get you out of here." Without waiting for an answer, he pulled her off the bed, marching her in the direction of her dressing room.

Abby shook off the large hand wrapped about her upper arm. "I really do appreciate what you did, Mr.—"

"Garrett," he interjected, putting his hand on her back as he continued directing her across the studio lot.

Apollo Studios took up several acres of prime Los Angeles real estate and as he appeared to know exactly where he was going, Abby wondered if he worked for the studio in some capacity. No, she determined instantly, after working here for five years, she had at least a nodding acquaintance with everyone employed by Apollo. And she knew she'd never seen this Mr. Garrett before. He was not the type of man one would easily forget.

She stopped in her tracks. "Well, as I was saying, I really appreciate you stepping in like that, but I'm fine now. I don't need you to accompany me to my dressing room."

He didn't budge. "I think you do."

"Really," she protested, "despite what you might think about Jessica Thorne, Abby Swan does not invite men into her dressing room."

"You could have been killed," he pointed out with deadly accuracy. "Or hasn't that gotten through your head yet?"

Remembering the dent the light had made in the floor, only inches from her head, Abby experienced a burst of fear-inspired adrenaline. "Accidents happen," she snapped.

"Sure they do. And sometimes you're lucky enough to have someone push you out of the way of them."

Touché, she admitted inwardly. "You're right," she said in a conciliatory tone. "You did save my life and I'm very appreciative, Mr. Garrett."

"Of course you are." He slanted her a strange, almost secretive smile as if waiting for her to say something else.

Of course, Abby realized. Nobody in Hollywood was *that* altruistic. "I suppose I do owe you something," she murmured thoughtfully, wondering how one went about setting a value on one's own life.

"Do you believe in the old adage that states once you save a life it's yours?"

Abby would have thought he was flirting with her were it not for the hardness of his eyes. "I'm willing to pay a reward, Mr. Garrett, but you're asking a bit too much."

"How do you know? I haven't even set a price yet."

His tone was too quiet, his tawny eyes too calm. Sam Garrett looked as if he knew a secret about her that he wasn't prepared to reveal. Abby grew decidedly uneasy.

"Look, I've had a long day. Just name your price and I'll write you a check."

"I don't want money." His words did nothing to instill confidence.

"I see," she said, not seeing anything at all. Who was this man? And what was he doing on a soundstage that was supposed to be closed?

"I'd like to take you to dinner."

"I'm sorry, but I'm not in the habit of going to dinner with strangers, Mr. Garrett."

Sam's original plan had been to wait until the taping was finished, then take Abby out to dinner, explaining the situation to her privately. Knowing she was, despite her public image, a very private person, a restaurant had seemed the perfect place to tell her of Jordan Winston's worries. She probably wouldn't believe him right away, but she also wouldn't risk a scene by marching out after declaring his revelation too fanciful for words.

The idea that someone was trying to kill Abby Swan was admittedly ludicrous, Sam agreed. But he had come to the unwilling conclusion that that was precisely the case. And if this latest incident with the light was any indication, time was running out. She had to listen to what he had to say. But damn it, he considered, glancing around at the bustling activity on the lot, this was not the place.

"Call me Sam," he instructed with a smile that didn't quite reach his eyes. "And don't forget, I just saved your neck, Abby. I felt those soft curves along every inch of my body and I held you while you trembled in my arms. Now how can you call us strangers?"

There was a quiet, compelling force about him that held Abby momentarily spellbound as she searched his smooth amber gaze. This was not a man who took rejection lightly if, indeed, he accepted it at all.

She looked pointedly down at her clothing. "I'm not exactly prepared to go out."

"I'll wait while you change."

Abby had the feeling he'd wait until doomsday, if that's what it took. He possessed an aura of patient authority that she could almost see. Shaking off that fanciful thought, Abby tried again. "I have other plans."

"Break them."

"I will not," she retorted with a false show of bravado.

Sam liked the way her flash of irritation brightened her soft gray eyes to a brilliant silver. He enjoyed a bit of temper in a woman; it pointed to other, more enjoyable passions. Reminding himself that he couldn't allow Abby's innate sensuality to sidetrack him, he crossed his arms over his chest and gazed down at her.

Abby told herself that she was a fool even to be considering his invitation. She knew nothing about this man. He'd suddenly appeared on a closed soundstage, as if he'd materialized from thin air, and although he admittedly saved her life, he seemed to be insisting on something far more than a simple dinner invitation. Of course he hadn't come right out and said anything that she could put a finger on, but this Sam Garrett, whoever he was, had hidden depths. Of that much she was certain.

"I'm only asking for dinner, Abby. Not a lifetime commitment," he stated with a mildly sardonic smile.

"What are you doing here?" she asked with honest interest. "This is supposed to be a closed soundstage."

"I've always found artificial barriers a bit of a challenge."

She arched an ebony eyebrow. "Meaning that you're nothing but a simple gate-crasher?"

"What do you think?" he countered with a question of his own.

Abby privately thought that there was not a single simple thing about this man. She was appalled to find herself growing more fascinated the longer they carried on this conversation. A thread of self-interest assured her that he would not be as easily manipulated as the men she usually went out with. While Abby liked a challenge, she wasn't foolhardy, either.

"I'm too tired to think anything," she complained. "I'm sorry, Mr. Garrett, but I've had a long day and I really would like to change my clothes and go home."

"I thought you said you had a date."

"That isn't any of your concern," she pointed out briskly. "Now, if you'll excuse me, as much as I've enjoyed this little chat, I really have to go." She turned away, secretly surprised he'd been so willing to allow her escape. "Oh," she said, looking back over her shoulder, "if you'll leave your address with my secretary, I'll have her send you a check."

Sam experienced a burst of irritation as he viewed *Potomac*'s director watching them with undisguised interest. No, he decided reluctantly, this was definitely not the place for a life-and-death discussion. He'd have to bide his time while continuing to keep an eye on her.

"Don't bother." Sam waved away her offer, then surprised Abby by appearing to drop the subject altogether. "I'll be seeing you around," he stated before sauntering off in the direction of the set.

Abby watched him go, wondering why his words had held the odd ring of a threat. *Ridiculous*, she assured herself. *Your imagination is simply working overtime.*

Once in her dressing room, she picked up the telephone receiver, pressing the plastic buttons with oddly shaking fingers. While she waited on hold, she began to wipe off the heavy theatrical makeup, becoming less anxious as she hummed along with Placido Domingo. One thing about Swan Pharmaceuticals, they had the classiest Muzak in town.

"Abby," the male voice finally came onto the line, "you must be psychic. I was just thinking of calling you. I need to make reservations; what time do you want to eat?"

Despite her lingering discomfort with Sam Garrett's sudden appearance, Abby returned the smile she heard in Kenneth Swan's voice. One thing she could always count on from her half brother was his ability to cheer her up.

"I'm sorry, Ken, but Jessica had a rough day and Abby wants nothing more than to drag the woman's bloody body home and soak it in a hot tub."

"I suppose that leaves me to an intimate little dinner with Kristin," he stated, naming the latest in a long line of tall, willowy blondes he had dated. "So Jessica got it today, did she?" he asked with friendly interest. "Where?"

"In bed, where else?" Abby quipped. "I swear she's the only lobbyist in Washington who deducts her satin sheets as a business expense."

"Don't count on it," he advised. "Not every politician is as upstanding as our favorite pillar of morality, Jordan Winston."

Abby smiled at the mention of her godfather. "I really am sorry about dinner," she apologized. "But it hasn't been one of my better days."

"What happened?" he asked, his voice instantly alert.

"One of the overhead lights fell down and almost scalped me."

"You mean Jessica," he corrected.

"No, I mean me. This wasn't in the script, Ken. A light broke loose from the scaffolding and Sam knocked me out of the way just in time."

"Sam?"

"Sam Garrett," Abby elaborated, a little curious herself why she thought of him by his first name. He certainly hadn't invited any feelings of intimacy.

"Abby," Ken suggested patiently, "why don't you back up a little. Who the hell is Sam Garrett?"

She'd like to know the very same thing. "Just someone who happened to be on the soundstage."

"I thought Griffen was going to shut it down for the final episode."

"He was. He did," she corrected.

"Then what was this Garrett guy doing there?"

She shrugged. "He said something about challenges," she mumbled. "Oh, let's not talk about it anymore," she decided firmly. "Hey, guess what?"

Ken sounded distracted. "What?"

"Although I know it'll break your heart to lose your roommate," she said with a chuckle, "the workmen finally finished up today. So you can have your bed back, brother dear, and I can quit feeling guilty about the crimp I've been putting in your social life."

"I've enjoyed your company, kiddo," he assured her. "Are you sure you don't want to go out? My treat."

"No thanks, you have your intimate little dinner with Kristin. I'll just spend the evening with a tubful of bubbles and a racy novel."

Ken's tone lowered. "I worry about you, Abby. You didn't used to be this accident-prone."

"I've had a lot on my mind," Abby murmured, as if that would explain the rash of near-fatal accidents she'd experienced lately. Her voice thickened slightly. "Do you know, Kenneth Swan, the day I found you was the luckiest day of my life."

"Mine, too," he agreed swiftly. "Now promise me you'll be careful."

Abby experienced a rush of love at her brother's caring tone. Whenever she thought about how Matthew Swan's actions had cost her twenty-nine years with her brother, it was difficult not to hate her stubborn, autocratic father.

"I promise," she said. "Have fun tonight," she added unnecessarily.

"Kristin's always fun," he agreed absently. "Take care, Abby," he warned softly as he hung up.

Abby changed quickly and managed to avoid questions from the rest of the crew as she made her way to the parking lot. She suddenly felt a lot like a kid taking off for summer recess. Not that she was going to have time for recreation, she reminded herself firmly. She was going to get the money to produce her film if it was the last thing she did.

So intent was she on that thought, Abby failed to notice the tall man following her from a discreet distance, a slight limp marring his purposeful stride. Before she had reached her car, he stopped to carry on a low conversation with another individual. The second man was shorter and distinctly older, but his clear blue eyes were still young and alert.

"She turned me down," Sam explained by way of greeting.

A pewter-gray eyebrow climbed the weathered face. "You gotta be kidding! Sam Garrett striking out? That's a first."

Sam granted a wry smile. "Not exactly," he admitted. "But I will admit she threw me a bit of a curve. Especially since I'd just saved her stubborn neck."

The elder man's grin faded. "Another accident?"

"Yeah." Sam's answer was brief and heavy with disbelief. "Keep a close eye on her tonight, okay Johnny?"

Sam had worked with Johnny O'Neill on several occasions before the older man had retired. Thinking that his old friend might be finding retirement a bit dull, he'd asked for his assistance with around-the-clock surveillance of Abby Swan. Johnny, not surprisingly, had jumped at the chance.

"Of course I will," Johnny answered immediately. "By the way, I'm sorry about last night, but with Ernie out somewhere in the middle of the Pacific, Mary needed me to take her to the hospital. I'll bet spending a foggy night cramped up in your car didn't do a helluva lot for that leg."

"Don't worry about it," Sam dismissed the other man's concern with the impatience of someone not used to dealing with illness or injuries. Then he grimaced and raked a hand through his hair. "Hell, I forgot to ask—boy or girl?"

"A girl. Samantha Jayne Stevens. You know, I always thought those old geezers who wanted to pass the photos and brag about their grandkids were a crock," Johnny admitted with a wide grin. "But all of a sudden I understand. I felt like busting all my buttons when that little girl made her appearance."

Sam smiled, a genuine smile that transformed his craggy features. "Did you say Mary named her Samantha?"

"Of course. Mary's always adored you, Sam. There was a time I thought you might even end up my son-in-law."

"Until she was swept off her feet by a guy in uniform," Sam reminded him. Although there had never been anything romantic between him and Mary O'Neill, Sam had been aware of Johnny's hopes and had been relieved when the woman he'd always thought of as a little sister had fallen in love with the handsome young Navy lieutenant from San Diego.

"Ernie's a good kid," Johnny acknowledged, nodding his silvery head topped with a blue Dodgers' cap. At that moment, Abby's car pulled out of her designated parking space and both men returned to business. "Gotta go," the proud new grandfather muttered. "Oh, I almost forgot." He tossed Sam a cigar as he got into his car.

Sam's grin of thanks faded as he watched Abby drive off with Johnny O'Neill trailing at a discreet distance. Then, heaving a deep sigh, he climbed into his own car, determined to go home and get some sleep. He was getting too old for twenty-four-hour surveillances, he considered grimly. In that respect, maybe this new desk job everyone was urging him to take wasn't such a bad idea.

THE MOMENT ABBY ARRIVED HOME, she went straight into the kitchen, her judicious gaze taking in the restoration. They'd done an excellent job. No one would ever suspect that only a month ago this cheery room had been gutted by flames.

She opened a few cupboards, belatedly remembering that she'd have to restock the shelves. There was nothing in the house to eat. Not that she was hungry. Fatigue, as well as the latest accident, had served to dull her appetite.

She twisted a faucet, pleased to see the plumbing had been reconnected. The last she'd heard, the plumber's bad back was acting up again and he wasn't certain he'd be able to finish up before the weekend. Next she turned on the range-top burners, watching each redden to a warm glow. How on earth could she have left that burner on before going to bed? She was usually far more efficient than that.

Abby sighed, realizing that her mind had obviously been elsewhere that night. And she knew exactly where. All those dead ends she'd experienced trying to get funding for her film. She was simply going to have to be more careful in the future, or she wouldn't be around to produce the thing when the money did come through.

Turning off all the burners, she made her way upstairs to the bedroom, tossing her clothing onto a chair in the corner. Gratefully she climbed between the sheets. She was tired, every bone in her body ached, and someone was banging away with a jackhammer inside her head. When she'd gotten out of bed this morning, Abby had had high hopes for the day. She'd planned to wrap up another season's shooting of *Potomac* and have dinner with Ken. Afterwards, she'd go home to a nice glass of wine and some music while she reread the screenplay for *Medicine Woman*, the film she intended come hell or high water to produce, direct and star in.

Instead, the shooting had dragged on far later than planned and she'd almost ended up under a huge klieg light. That unpleasant memory brought up the image of Sam Garrett. Who was he? And what had he been doing on a closed soundstage? As grateful as she was for his fortuitous appearance, she had a vague, uneasy feeling that she hadn't seen the last of him. That thought made her both excited and apprehensive at the same time.

Exhaling a soft, frustrated breath, she gave up on the problem for the moment, surrendering to her exhaustion as she fell into a deep, dreamless sleep.

Meanwhile, across the sprawling city, the object of all her curiosity sat in the dark, puffing thoughtfully on a long dark cigar. Despite the fact he'd been without sleep for over twenty-four hours, Sam couldn't expunge the picture of Abby Swan from his mind.

He'd spent the past two weeks following her, remaining in the shadows as he'd observed her, studied her, learned every nuance of her behavior. He knew how her teeth worried her full bottom lip when she was upset, how she twisted her hair around her fingers while concentrating, how she always crossed her fingers behind her back before shooting a scene.

He knew her infectious laughter could strike a chord deep within him, and while her performance as the sultry Jessica Thorne called out to the primitive side of his masculinity, he wanted even more to make love to the vibrant woman behind that sexy image. He'd become as obsessed with Abby Swan as the man trying to kill her, Sam realized.

"Lunacy," he muttered, knowing that a relationship with the woman was out of the question.

They came from different worlds. His consisted of long, often boring hours of hard work, hers was a world of glitter and fame. He made a comfortable living, she had more millions at her fingertips than most third world nations. He struggled down here on the ground, while she soared like an eagle. Hell, the chances of Abby Swan settling for a guy like Sam Garrett were pretty remote. It was a nice fantasy, but it wasn't going to happen.

He shook his head, not at all happy with the errant thoughts he'd been having lately. They weren't professional and Sam Garrett was first and foremost a professional. He didn't like the way Abby had gotten under his skin. He didn't like it at all. Disgusted with his behavior, he ground out the cigar, determining that from here on in, he wasn't going to allow these uncharacteristic flights of fantasy.

"And if you believe that," he muttered, falling onto his bed, still fully dressed, "I've got some swampland in Florida I'll sell you for a song."

2

THE STRIDENT DEMAND of the telephone shattered the dark silence and Abby reached over, fumbling for the receiver.

"Hello?" she mumbled.

"Abby, we've got problems," Lance Griffen stated without preamble.

Abby narrowed her eyes, focusing on the luminous dial of her clock radio. Surely *Potomac*'s director wasn't calling at this hour simply to push his case concerning her contract talks once more?

"Lance, do you have any idea what time it is?"

"We've lost the tape," he stated grimly without answering her question.

Abby sat up in bed, pushing her hair from her eyes. "Lost? What does that mean?"

"It means that damn incompetent the union sent over to replace Pauline erased an entire day's shooting. We'll have to do it again."

"Oh, no," she groaned. "I thought we'd wrapped everything up for this season."

"Don't feel like the Lone Ranger," he shot back. "You're not the only one inconvenienced, Abby. I was supposed to start directing a network miniseries tomorrow. Do you have any idea how many people have to be notified before morning?"

"I'm sorry," she murmured. "I know this isn't easy on anyone. What time?"

"Makeup's at seven."

Abby stifled another groan. "I'll be there."

"Of course you will."

He hung up abruptly, leaving Abby to stare at the receiver, wishing she believed in astrology. She'd love to discover that all this was happening simply because her stars, or her planets, or whatever were in the wrong phase. Sighing, she set her clock radio to come on at five-thirty, then closed her eyes, trying to go back to sleep. This time, however, she was less than successful, and when the cheery voice of the morning deejay filled the still-darkened room, Abby crawled out of bed, feeling as if she'd just gone ten rounds with Mohammed Ali in his prime.

All her bones ached as she stood under the warm shower, lifting her face to the pulsating spray. As she toweled herself dry, she saw bruises that hadn't been there yesterday morning and knew they were the result of Sam Garrett's body crashing into hers.

Abby couldn't get rid of the odd feeling that Sam's appearance on the set at precisely that moment had not been a fortunate coincidence. All during the love scene, she'd experienced a vague sense of discomfort, as if she were being watched. But she was always uncomfortable taping Jessica's bedroom scenes in front of the crew, and at the time, she'd attributed her uneasiness to that. This morning, she was beginning to wonder.

"I'm going to make certain Lance is more diligent about closing the soundstage today," she said aloud as she dressed in a pair of cream linen slacks and a red blouse. "One thing I definitely don't need is another encounter with that man."

Across the sprawling city, Sam was already on his third cup of coffee when the telephone rang. "She's on the move," Johnny O'Neill informed him without wasting time on polite preliminaries.

Sam muttered a low, harsh oath. "I thought for certain she'd sleep in."

"So did I. But the tape got fouled up last night and they're having to reshoot. She left the house so fast I didn't have time to call you until I knew where she was going to light."

"So you're at the studio?"

"Yep. She went into makeup at seven, they should begin taping any time."

"Keep an eye on her," Sam instructed needlessly. "I'll be there as soon as I can."

Damn, he considered furiously as he threw on his clothes. If anything happened to Abby Swan, he'd never forgive himself.

THE TAPING WENT WITHOUT A HITCH, something Abby was personally grateful for. She'd been undeniably nervous, casting surreptitious glances up at the resecured light, waiting unreasonably for it to fall again.

She had just entered her dressing room when there was a knock at the door.

"Abby? Are you in there?"

"Come on in," she answered instantly, recognizing the voice of her friend and secretary.

"It went well," the petite redhead commented as she entered the motor home.

"Thanks. I hate shooting retakes, though. It reminds me of eating leftover oatmeal."

"Well, that scene *was* pretty mushy."

"Your puns get worse every year."

Abby grimaced, glancing at the handful of envelopes the woman carried. She'd hired Kate Britton five years ago, when she'd begun getting more letters than she could answer herself. Now the weekly fan mail was too much for either woman to handle. The network had been forced to hire three secretaries to answer everything from requests for autographed pictures, to hate mail from women who viewed the television vamp as a threat to the institution of marriage. Kate served as overseer, pulling letters she felt Abby would want to see.

"Anything interesting?"

Kate leafed through a slim stack of envelopes. "Still nothing from lover boy," she assured Abby, referring to one obsessed fan who had proven more and more distracting over the past season. "It's all pretty much run-of-the-mill. Here's a request for a donation to the Big Sisters celebrity fund-raising auction."

"Of course I'll send something. What did I give them last year?"

"That slinky negligee you wore to seduce the head of the Armed Services Committee. I heard that it was their most popular item. Even better than JR's cowboy hat."

"Everyone loves a villain," Abby mused with a smile. "Let's see, we want to do just as well this year...." She fell silent, considering some of the outrageous outfits her character had worn during the season.

"I know! If the cleaner can get the stain out, we'll give them this." She opened the robe, displaying the crimson slip that caressed her curves like a second skin.

"Uh-uh." Kate vetoed the idea immediately.

"Why not?"

"Look, if you don't come back to the show, the writers are going to kill you off. Remember, that's what that shooting was all about today."

"So?"

"So, if you get your funding for *Medicine Woman* and don't return, that slip will be worth even more with the fake bloodstain on it."

"You might be right," Abby conceded, putting her feet up on a glass topped table as she leaned back in her chair. She massaged her neck wearily. "That idea is just gross enough to be worth a fortune."

"In that respect, it's a bit like *Potomac*," Kate offered dryly.

Abby groaned. "Don't remind me. If I don't find the money for my project this summer, I don't know what I'm going to do. Steve Marshall was only willing to option his book to me for two years and that's nearly up."

In fact, she reflected, the Pulitzer Prize author had been amazingly patient, considering the offers he must have received for the movie rights to his novel. Abby had written the screenplay during her hiatus from *Potomac* last year. Since then she'd been searching for funding, finding door after door closed to new projects. Meanwhile Abby had received several film offers but every one had demonstrated the perils of typecasting. All the characters were carbon copies of Jessica Thorne—offering glitter, but no substance.

Her option would run out in August, three months from now. Then, if she hadn't begun the film, she was scheduled to return for a sixth season, a thought that was becoming more depressing every day. Time was definitely running out.

"Aren't you looking forward to playing a geriatric vamp? From the way *Potomac* tops the ratings year after year, you could probably stay on the show forever."

"Now I know why you're my best friend," Abby shot back, tossing a gray suede pillow at her. "You're so terrific at cheering me up.... Come in," she answered the knock on the door.

Kate's and Abby's shared laughter dropped off as the door swung opened and Sam Garrett entered the motor home.

"You again." Abby stared at him, wondering how he'd managed to breach the additional security Lance had put on the soundstage.

"You know what they say about bad pennies."

"Who are you?"

"I told you that yesterday," he reminded her.

"What are you doing here?"

"FBI business," he stated nonchalantly.

Kate half rose from the couch. "I think that's my exit cue."

"You don't have to leave," Abby answered instantly. Her eyes shifted from the overtly curious face of her friend to Sam Garrett's inscrutable gaze. "Anything you have to say to me, Mr. Garrett, you can say in front of Kate."

A slight flicker of annoyance appeared in his eyes, but with a shrug of his shoulders, Sam decided to give Abby this one.

He turned toward the other woman, extending his hand. "Sam Garrett, FBI."

Kate was practically melting right on the spot, Abby considered, watching her friend gaze up at Sam. She felt an odd flash of something she vaguely recognized as jealousy. *Don't be ridiculous*, she scolded herself. *You don't even particularly like the man.* Still, Abby was unreasonably irritated as Kate seemed in no hurry to retrieve her hand from Sam's grasp.

"Kate Britton," Kate stated, her eyes sparkling. "Available."

Sam's gaze lit with masculine acknowledgment of Kate's less-than-subtle invitation. His investigation had uncovered the fact that while she was discreet in her relationships with men, Kate Britton maintained an attitude identical to his own. She preferred her relationships without strings, without commitment on either side. Sam knew Kate's offer had been issued in earnest. Yet, he considered, as enticing as the voluptuous redhead was, she didn't affect him with the same jolt as Abby.

"I'll keep that in mind," he answered smoothly. "Now, can we have that little talk?" he said, turning to Abby.

His words were couched as a request, but Abby recognized it for what it was. An order. Softly spoken, but written in stone nonetheless.

"I suppose I don't have any choice," she muttered.

"You called that one right," he agreed negligently as he took a seat on the couch. His eyes left hers to circle the interior of Abby's dressing room, taking in the molded black suede furniture and modernistic chrome tables. "This place looks like something out of Buck Rogers."

"I'm told it's the height of sophistication," she countered.

As Abby's gray gaze swept over the room, she recalled how she'd initially hated the way her comfortable motor home had been transformed. Black was the predominant color; the walls had been covered with silver and black metallic wallpaper, and black vases held a fresh supply of lilies, whose scent never failed to give her a headache by the end of the day.

When she'd attempted to voice a complaint, the decorator had run to the head of the studio, who explained in no uncertain terms that they were building an image for Jessica Thorne. One Abby would be well advised to accept.

"It *is* a little like walking into a time machine," she admitted, "but I don't even notice it anymore."

"How can you spend most of your waking hours in a place so alien to your personality?"

Abby shrugged as she opened the refrigerator, taking out two cans of Coke, one of which she handed to Kate. When she offered a third to him, Sam declined with a shake of his head.

"I didn't know FBI agents were so skilled in pop analysis," she commented, pulling the tab on the aluminum can. "Tell me, Mr. Garrett, what type of dressing room do *you* see me living in?"

"Something like your beach house," he said instantly, not having to give the matter a moment's thought. "Simply decorated, lots of bright primary colors, floral prints. Natural. Like you."

She lowered the can from her lips. "How do you know about my beach house?"

Sam hesitated briefly, then replied, "I've been keeping an eye on you since the fire."

Abby's gaze narrowed. "Why?"

His mouth firmed into a hard, forbidding line. "Because Jordan Winston doesn't think it was an accident."

She frowned, running her finger around the rim of the can. Jordan Winston had been her father's best friend and he was her godfather. She was grateful for his concern, but where had he gotten such an idea?

"I don't understand."

Sam leaned forward, his elbows on his knees, his fingers linked between his legs. The man had nice fingers, Abby noted irrelevantly. They were long and well tapered, his nails square cut.

"Jordan thinks it has something to do with those letters you've been receiving."

His casually stated words caught her off guard and she sought an excuse, any excuse, to stall for time. Did this man know everything about her? The letters from an anonymous fan who seemed to have confused Abby with her screen image, vowing that if he couldn't have her, he wouldn't allow any other man the opportunity, had become admittedly bothersome; that's why she'd mentioned them to Jordan. But what had made him connect those letters with her rash of accidents? She wondered suddenly if this man might actually be the individual writing the letters.

"May I see your identification?"

"Sure. For a while there I didn't think you were going to ask. That would've been dumb, Abby. You shouldn't trust anyone at this point." He reached into a jacket pocket.

Despite her irritation at his superior tone, Abby was drawn to the hard, lean lines of the body so well defined by the fitted white shirt, but then her attention was arrested by what else the navy jacket had concealed.

"You're wearing a gun."

"And you're wearing one sexy slip," he countered calmly.

Glancing down, Abby realized the robe had separated, giving him a clear view of her body under the filmy crimson silk. She pulled the robe closed.

"I suppose that statement is suppose to have some significance?"

His hard mouth curved slightly and Abby found herself waiting with anticipation for a smile that didn't come. "Tools of the trade," he answered politely. "I have mine and you have yours."

Abby tugged the sash of the robe even tighter. "My slip is a far cry from a gun."

"Oh, I don't know," he said laconically, "I'd say it's every bit as dangerous. In its own way."

Ignoring Kate's muffled intake of breath at the sexual implication in Sam's husky voice, Abby searched his eyes for a spark of flirtation that would match his provocative words. Nothing. No humor, no warmth, no interest. Just those steady topaz eyes that made her feel as if she were being examined under a microscope.

"I believe you were showing me your identification," she reminded him firmly.

"I was. Until you got sidetracked checking out my gun."

From Sam's dry tone, Abby had the uneasy feeling he was aware of her prolonged study of his body, before her attention had been captured by his weapon.

"I'm not used to men with guns lounging about my dressing room."

"That's a relief," he drawled, pulling out a leather folder that he flipped open with one hand and passed to her.

He appeared younger than his picture, but Abby would recognize that scowl anywhere. "Don't you ever smile?" She returned the identification.

"Not on duty," he answered immediately. "It's bad for the image."

Abby stared at him for a moment, frustrated by those deep, expressionless eyes. "Is that a joke?"

"Of course not. Joking is definitely off limits while on duty. Would *you* trust your life to a joker?"

Although she suspected Sam Garrett was teasing her, his words were deadly serious. "Is that what you want **me** to do?"

He replaced the folder with a restraint of movement that had Abby momentarily fascinated. "No," he answered simply.

"Oh. Then why are you here?"

"I *expect* you to do it," he corrected. "From now on, until we catch your ardent pen pal, you're not going to make a single move that I don't approve ahead of time."

His calm self-assurance that she'd acquiesce to his arrogant demand immediately sparked rebellion. "If you think I'm going to agree to that," she said, turning away to reach for a large jar of cold cream, "you're crazier than the loony-tune writing me those letters."

"Abby," Kate advised, "you can at least listen to what the man has to say."

Sam threw Abby's own words back at her. "Then you'll admit the guy is unbalanced."

She shrugged uncaringly. "Look, I get a lot of letters from people who mistake me for Jessica Thorne. One little old lady started hitting me with her purse last week in the supermarket. She wanted me to quit blackmailing poor Senator Bradshaw. . . . It goes with the territory."

"How many letters do you get threatening your life?"

"Not many," she admitted. Slathering her face with thick cold cream, she refused to meet his eyes. "So, if you believe he's a real threat, why don't you just run along and find the guy?"

Sam experienced a fleeting moment of attraction that was not entirely unexpected. She was, after all, a beautiful woman. Even with that junk spread all over her face.

"You know, Abby," he drawled sapiently, "I've always admired bravery, but let me warn you, sweetheart, you keep up this attitude and you'll end up the gutsiest corpse in the morgue."

His casual tone inexplicably made the words seem even more threatening, and Abby risked a look at him in the mirror. "You don't pull any punches, do you?"

"I can't afford to."

"Do you really believe that light was rigged to fall on me?"

"What light?" Kate asked, her startled gaze moving back and forth between Sam's hard-set face and Abby's defiant one.

"I didn't think it worth mentioning," Abby explained as she started wiping the cold cream off her face. "A light fell during yesterday's taping, that's all. It was just an accident."

"Like all the others," Kate murmured. "But you don't think it was an accident?" she asked Sam.

"I know it wasn't; the bolts were sheared, but not due to any wear and tear."

Abby still couldn't believe him. "And the fire? And my tanks? You don't think they were accidents, either?"

He rose, jamming his hands into his back pockets. "I didn't agree with Jordan at first," he admitted. "But I've changed my mind."

"What changed your opinion?" she asked curiously.

He studied Abby silently, wondering how much she should know at this point. Her state of undress was driving him crazy; Sam had never been attracted to a woman as he was to this one.

"We'll talk over dinner," he promised. "Right now you'd better put some clothes on before I forget what I'm supposed to be here for."

Abby stared at him. Had that been an honest sign of male interest? His steady amber gaze revealed nothing. So what else was new? Although his gleaming eyes caused her to grip the lapels of the robe a little tighter, Abby held her ground.

"I'm not going out with you. I thought we'd settled that yesterday."

"Of course you are," he said in a self-assured tone that only served to irritate Abby further.

"Over my dead body," she retorted furiously.

"That's precisely what we're trying to avoid," he said, ignoring Kate's slight gasp. "Now, do you change, or do I drag you out to the car like that?"

"In case you've forgotten, Mr. Garrett, this is the United States and you work for the FBI, not the gestapo." She got up and went over to her closet. "Now, if you'd don't mind, I'd like some privacy so I can get dressed and go home. Alone," she tacked on pointedly. Grabbing her clothing from the rack, she marched into the bathroom, slamming the door behind her.

Kate had been watching the exchange with wide-eyed fascination. Now, apparently deciding that discretion was called for, she rose from the black sofa and went over to the closed door.

"Look, Abby, as much as I'd love to stay for round three, I've got a date tonight. I'll call you tomorrow, okay?"

"Sure," Abby responded, trying to keep the distress from her voice. The one thing she didn't want was to be left alone with Sam Garrett. "Have fun."

"You, too," Kate trilled merrily, leaving the motor home. As she reached the bottom step, she turned, looking up at the man standing in the doorway. "For Abby's sake, I hope you're way off base about those letters, Sam Garrett, FBI," she stated thoughtfully. "But she's needed someone like you for a long time." She grinned, accepting defeat with inherent good humor. "Good luck."

Sam inclined his head in acknowledgment. "Thanks. I think."

Kate's laughter followed her as she made her way across the lot. Sam watched her leave, then settled down on the couch. He was a patient man, having honed that personality trait through years of seeking the single needle in a haystack that would break a case wide open. The only time he'd succumbed to impatience was this last time he'd been in the hospital. He'd thought he was going to go crazy, locked up in that white room for all those months.

But he hadn't. He'd survived, as he always did. And now relying on that patience once again, he'd wait for Abby Swan. For as long as it took.

Taking advantage of the privacy offered by the small bathroom, Abby picked up the telephone, dialing the Washington D.C. number of Jordan Winston, only to have his answering service state that he was unavailable. So much for that, she thought with a sigh, slipping into the slacks and blouse she'd worn this morning. After she'd dallied as long as humanly possible, she exited the bathroom, not particularly surprised to see Sam Garrett seated casually on her sofa, appearing perfectly at home.

"Don't you have something important you're supposed to be doing?" she demanded.

Good Lord, she was beautiful, he considered not for the first time. Although nearly the entire male population lusted after Jessica Thorne, the first time Sam had viewed Abby Swan without her theatrical trappings he'd been struck by a natural beauty possessed by very few women. Her hair was a thick, smooth ebony, falling below her shoulders. Her eyes were a clear gray that became alive with silver lights when she was happy. She had incredible bone structure, the kind of face made to be loved by a camera.

After checking out the information he'd been given by Jordan Winston, Sam would have taken on this case for his old friend even if Abby Swan wasn't the most stunning woman he'd ever seen. But he had to admit, it had been a long time since a job had offered such pleasant scenery.

"What could be more important than waiting to take television's sexiest villainess out to dinner?" he asked easily.

Abby wasn't about to succumb to the charm he'd suddenly turned on. She didn't even like this man. Correction, she refused to allow herself to like him. He was too bossy, too sure of himself. Too male.

She frowned at him. "I don't know, whatever you G-men do. Tracking down bank robbers, gangsters, that sort of thing."

"That stuff is old hat," he responded lazily. "I've never played bodyguard to a sex symbol before. While you're not the easiest assignment I've ever drawn, Abby, it's bound to do wonders for my image around the agency."

"What are you talking about?"

"I'm afraid you and I are stuck with each other until we catch the guy writing you those letters."

"Are you saying that you're my own personal body-guard?"

Sam shrugged. "That's about it."

"I didn't realize the FBI provided those services." Her questioning tone invited comment.

"There are certain perks to being Senator Jordan Winston's goddaughter," he stated simply.

Abby sighed, wondering when Jordan would realize she was a grown woman, capable of taking care of herself. Jordan Winston and his wife, Emily, had always played an important part in Abby's life. Karin Swan's Jaguar had overturned in a freak accident on the Santa Monica freeway when Abby was twelve, and Emily had immediately stepped in, playing a motherly role for Abby during her important teen years. While Jordan was legally the administrator of her trust fund, that would come to an end in three weeks, when she turned thirty and received control of Matthew Swan's estate. It was nice to be loved, she decided, but Jordan was taking all this far too seriously.

"Look, Mr. Garrett, I'm a bit old for a baby-sitter, so why don't you just mind your own business?"

"You are my business," he reminded her.

"You're out of your mind," she snapped, grabbing her purse from the table and marching toward the door. "Tell Jordan that I appreciate his concern, but I can take care of myself."

Abby didn't know how Sam did it; one minute he was lounging on the couch, the next he was standing over her.

"I can't let you go home alone, Abby," he said calmly.

"Damn it, Garrett," she hissed through clenched teeth, "I haven't done anything wrong. Even the FBI can't run around making prisoners out of ordinary citizens!"

"You're not a prisoner, Abby. You're in protective custody." Sam ignored her muttered response. "I don't care if you hate the idea," he added quietly. "Hell, I don't even care if you hate me. But I promised Jordan I'd keep you alive and I'm not about to go back on my word."

"I can see I've been a little naive about the inner workings of the Washington establishment. Tell me, do all senators have their own FBI lackeys? Or is Jordan one of the lucky ones?" Knowing that she'd overstepped her bounds, Abby looked away, already regretting her words.

"Anything else?"

Abby cast a cautious glance his way, afraid of what she'd find. His tawny eyes were observing her in a steady, but unmistakably dangerous way.

"What?" she asked softly.

"Do you want to take any other shots at me before we leave here? Any slurs on my family tree? Feel like casting any more unsavory aspersions on my profession? My intellect? My manhood?" His even tone held a tinge of cold hard steel.

"Why don't you try that one," he suggested. "Like most men, I'll admit to a few hidden doubts and fears. Dig a little deeper and you'll probably be able to uncover enough to tip the scales in your favor for a time. A very short time." A warning flashed momentarily in his eyes. "Take your best shot, sweetheart."

Abby realized that Sam Garrett could be pushed just so far and knew she'd come dangerously close to overstepping that boundary.

"I'm sorry," she murmured, "I shouldn't have said that."

When he didn't answer, Abby risked a glance upward, her breath catching in her throat as her gaze collided with his. Sam told himself that he should be furious at Abby for accusing him of compromising his ethics that way. While some of his methods might admittedly be described as unorthodox, no one could ever question his integrity. No one had ever dared until now. So why the hell did he feel like apologizing for that soft shadow darkening her eyes? Those lovely, lovely eyes.

"That's okay," he brusquely dismissed her behavior. "You've been under a lot of pressure lately. I suppose you're entitled to a few displays of temperament."

Abby was still staring at the harsh lines of his face, intrigued by the sensual warmth she'd seen gleaming in his eyes. Giving her head a quick toss, she grasped onto his words like a drowning man reaching for a lifeline. That's all it was, she told herself. She *had* been under a lot of strain lately. The scuba diving accident, the fire, trying to get the funding for her project, the pressure from both the network brass and her agent to sign a new contract for her continued appearance on *Potomac*.

Sam Garrett's reappearance had nothing to do with her mood swings this evening; he was simply the straw that broke the camel's back. That was all it was, she assured herself firmly, wishing she could honestly believe that.

3

ALTHOUGH ABBY KNEW she was probably asking for trouble, she balked one last time, more for show than anything else, before agreeing to leave the dressing room with Sam.

"I'd like to call Jordan," she insisted firmly.

"Fine. You can call him as soon as we get to your house."

"Why can't I check with him *before* you take me home?" she countered.

"Because," Sam replied patiently, "it's three hours later in Washington. As we stand here arguing, Jordan Winston is speaking at a banquet for the American Banking Association."

That was precisely the message his answering service had given her, Abby admitted secretly. "You really do know Jordan, don't you?"

Sam nodded. "Very well."

"And you came here today as a favor to him? Because both of you honestly think I'm in danger?"

"Right again."

She was not surprised Jordan would be concerned about her. But Abby was discomforted by the fact that he'd misused his position in the government on her behalf.

"Isn't that preferential treatment, Mr. Garrett?"

"I suppose some individuals might see it that way," he agreed calmly. "I prefer to think of it as returning a favor. Jordan Winston was instrumental in helping us conduct a successful investigation of a few less-than-admirable members of congress."

"A sting, you mean," she countered briskly.

Sam knew Abby was baiting him, trying to make him lose control so she'd gain the upper hand. For her own safety, he couldn't allow her that victory. She didn't have to like him, but she damn well had to respect his authority.

"I suppose it's all in how you see it," he returned equably. "Besides," he reminded her, "it just happens to be a federal crime to send death threats through the mail. We tend to take those things fairly seriously."

"What happens if I refuse to leave with you?"

"Then I'll have to carry you," he answered reasonably.

He was maddeningly self-assured. "You'd do that, wouldn't you?" she challenged hotly.

"And have a helluva good time while doing it," he agreed. Then his voice dropped and he leaned down, his words low and rumbling in her ear. "Don't push me, Abby," he warned softly, "or you may just end up with a lot more than you bargained for."

Before she could come up with an appropriate murderous response to his outrageous statement, Sam straightened, opening the door and inviting her outside with a nod of his head.

"Ready?"

"As if I had a choice," she muttered, marching past him with her head held high and her spine as stiff as a rod of cold steel.

"My car is parked in the lot," she stated as Sam led her to a nondescript blue American sedan.

"Not any more. I had it driven home for you."

"Why did you do that?"

"Because I didn't think you'd want to leave a 1959 Mercedes 300 SL roadster in the parking lot all night," he stated simply, opening the car door for her.

"I'm surprised you recognized it," Abby admitted as he climbed into the driver's seat and put the key in the ignition.

A dark brow rose as he turned toward her. "What's the matter, can't you imagine a guy who lives on a beer budget having champagne tastes?"

Abby thought she detected a note of sarcasm in his tone. "It was a birthday present," she stated briskly. "From my father, for my twenty-first birthday."

"Must be nice," he murmured, turning the key and putting his foot to the floor several times until the car reluctantly came to life. "My mom sent me a ski sweater for my last birthday. I'm hoping for a cap to match this year."

"My father enjoyed investing in cars," she snapped. "That's all it was. An investment."

He slanted her a curious glance. "Defensive, Abby?" he asked softly.

She folded her arms across her breasts. "Not at all," she professed. "Why should I be?"

"Beats me."

"Well, I'm not," she repeated firmly.

"Good. Because if that car makes you feel uncomfortable, I hate to think how you're going to feel with all those Swan millions in a few weeks."

"Do you know *everything* about me?" She didn't bother to conceal her frustration.

Sam glanced over at her as the car idled roughly at a stoplight. "Enough for now," he said simply. Then the light turned green and he returned his attention to the road.

It was not his words that suddenly had Abby feeling uneasy. It was what he had left unsaid. The implication that no matter how hard she tried to put some distance between herself and Sam Garrett, he wasn't going to be easily deterred from his original objective of staying close to her until the FBI found the person writing her those letters.

That idea was not a pleasant one. While she'd have to admit he certainly hadn't threatened her, there had been an unmistakable command in his deep, softly spoken words. Sam Garrett was used to calling the shots, that much was certain. She couldn't get that gun out of her mind and wondered if he'd ever killed a man.

Sam didn't miss the fleeting shadow that darkened Abby's eyes before she turned away, pretending an interest in the passing scenery.

"You okay?" he asked casually.

Abby warily glanced over at him, making a vast effort to clear her mind. He saw too much with those steady amber eyes.

"Sure," she answered blithely. "Why wouldn't I be? After all, I've had a terrific couple of days. I was almost killed, then some storm trooper forces his way into my life and tells me that I'm being stalked by some maniac and he's going to keep me under house arrest.

"Which," she added, "doesn't make me feel real secure, because I've the feeling my so-called protector is just as dangerous as whoever is writing me those letters."

His brow lifted in surprise. "Do you really see me as dangerous?"

She cocked her head, studying him thoughtfully. "Aren't you?"

"I've never really given it a lot of thought," he answered reflectively. "I suppose some people might find me irritating from time to time. And I'll admit to being opinionated and strong willed. But dangerous?" He shook his head. "I don't think so.... Are you afraid of me, Abby?" That was an interesting idea. Sam wouldn't have guessed Abby Swan could be frightened by anything or anyone.

"Are you kidding? Of course not." She met his questioning glance with an even gaze. "Matthew Swan's daughter isn't afraid of anything, Mr. Garrett. I'm surprised you didn't learn that while you were so busy researching every damn thing about my life."

Her acid tone didn't fool Sam for a minute. She was vulnerable. That, too, was a surprise. He'd developed an instinct for reading people; all too often his life had depended on that ability. And that intuitive sense told him that Abby was more complex a woman than she appeared at first glance. As he headed up the Pacific Coast highway, Sam decided some more questions were in order.

"What was your father like?" he asked, anxious to find the key.

Abby's answer was short and to the point. "Busy."

"And successful," he pointed out.

"I suppose so, if you consider the accumulation of vast sums of money as making a success of your life."

"Isn't that the usual yardstick?" he commented quietly. "Everyone may admire people like Gandhi and Mother Theresa, but let's face it, the Matthew Swans of the world have the real power."

His words were incredibly close to the tenets she'd heard her father espouse time and time again. "I don't want to talk about him."

"You brought him up in the first place," Sam reminded her.

"And now I'm dropping the subject, all right?"

He shrugged. "Sure. Although if it turns out your family connections have anything to do with these attempts on your life, we're going to have to talk about it," he warned.

She looked back at him curiously. "Why on earth would you even consider that? If you really believe my life is in jeopardy, it's that nut writing me the letters."

"Perhaps," he replied simply. "Perhaps not."

She shook her head. "If you're not dangerous, Garrett, you're crazy. Either way, I'm not wild about having you hovering over me."

"Would you do me a favor?" he asked suddenly.

"What?" she asked suspiciously, not trusting his casual tone.

"Would you call me Sam?"

"I don't think so," she said after a moment.

"Why not?"

"Because I only call my friends by their first names."

"And you're not about to consider me a friend," he guessed.

"Got it on the first try," she shot back.

"How about a compromise?"

Despite his amiable tone, Sam's eyes revealed his irritation. Abby realized that somehow she'd just gained the upper hand, weak as it was, and didn't feel inclined to give the man an inch.

"What do you have in mind?"

"Do you think you'd choke on 'hey, you'?"

His face was suddenly lit with humor, encouraging her to give in. Then he weakened her defenses even further by smiling. The grin was surprisingly boyish, softening the harsh lines of his face. His teeth were broad and white, and as her gaze moved upward, Abby watched, entranced, as his tawny eyes brightened to a brilliant gold. Lines she hadn't noticed earlier fanned out from those suddenly gorgeous eyes.

"You can smile," she stated nonsensically.

"Of course. What do you say, Abby? Is it a deal?"

Abby tried to repress her answering smile and failed. "I could probably manage that," she agreed.

He nodded, appearing inordinately pleased. "That's a start."

While Abby was admittedly impressed with Sam's choice of a restaurant, as he pulled the car into the parking lot, she wondered if he knew it was one of the most expensive in the valley. If this car was any example of his financial status, she was afraid the experience might prove embarrassing for him. Although his arrogant attitude had irritated her, Abby didn't like seeing anyone uncomfortable.

"This is one of my favorite places," she offered.

He pulled the key from the ignition. "I know."

"It has terrific food."

"So I hear."

"Then you haven't been here before?" she probed delicately.

He gave her an intent look. "What's the matter," he asked with deadly accuracy, "are you afraid you're going to end up washing dishes to pay for your dinner?"

Abby fought the telltale flush she could feel darkening her cheeks. "You're the one who was complaining about your so-called beer budget," she snapped back. "Well, the only beer in this place is imported. And expensive."

"Why don't you let me worry about that?"

She tossed her head. "Fine. I simply thought I should mention it."

"Consider it mentioned," he said, opening his door. Abby debated waiting, but decided against it. It wasn't much, but it was a rebellion of sorts, she thought, jumping out before he had the opportunity to come around and open her door.

The only sign of Sam's irritation was a slight narrowing of his eyes, but he refrained from commenting. As they entered the dimly lit restaurant, Abby was surprised to see the professionally stuffy maître d' break into a wide smile.

"Ms Swan, Sam, what a pleasure! I'm proud you've seen fit to honor us with your presence after such a long absence, Sam," he gushed with an enthusiasm that Abby, despite her charms, had never earned.

Sam returned the smile, and Abby was once again drawn to the warmth it radiated. "It's been too long, Max. How are you?"

The man's dark head bobbed. "Fine, fine. Thanks to you."

Sam's only response to the fervently stated praise was a slight nod of his head. "How's Martha?"

"Martha is the same as always. She'd love a chance to cook for you again. She's always complaining that no one can appreciate good food like Sam Garrett."

Sam chuckled. "Now that I'm back in L.A., I just might take you up on that," he agreed. "TV dinners lose their appeal after a while."

Max clucked his tongue. "You deserve better than plastic food served on aluminum trays." His eyes slid to Abby. "I think it's about time you settled down and found a wife to feed you."

"When I decide to get married, Max," Sam stated in a deep, husky tone, "cooking is going to be way down on my list of priorities." His gold eyes darkened with sexual insinuation as they moved to Abby.

She struggled against the quiet force that was holding her gaze to his. While she couldn't miss the deep intent in the bottom of the dark gold pools, it was even more disconcerting what the silent statement was doing to her body. Her pulse quickened, coming alive with a hunger that could not be satiated by anything on the royal-blue tasseled menus Max was holding. She could not control the answering desire that flooded into her own gray eyes and, reading it, Sam pressed his lips together into a grim, satisfied smile. Then he abruptly turned his attention to the avidly interested maître d'.

"Is our table ready, Max?"

The man's answering grin seemed almost as self-satisfied as Sam's had been. "Of course."

He turned away, leading Abby and Sam down the slight incline of carpeted stairs. Heads turned with interest as they walked past, something Abby had come to accept as inevitable. One reason she'd always enjoyed this restaurant was that its clientele was less likely to interrupt a meal, seeking autographs for nonexistent relatives. She knew, however, that tomorrow morning, the gossip line would be buzzing as people attempted to discover the identity of her tall, darkly formidable escort.

"As you requested," Max stated formally, having redonned his professional demeanor.

"It's perfect. Thank you," Sam responded, his own tone as formal as the maître d's.

Abby accepted the chair Max held out, waiting until after the wine steward had delivered a soft California Chardonnay to comment.

"If this table was any farther away from the others," she stated evenly as she unfolded the damask napkin and placed it on her lap, "we'd be eating dinner on the freeway."

"I thought a measure of privacy was in order."

She took a sip of wine, finding Sam's choice, surprisingly enough, to be superb. So much for pigeonholing the man with the beer drinkers of the world, she considered thoughtfully.

"If you're thinking of plying me with wine and filling my head with pretty phrases so you can seduce me later, it isn't going to work," she warned lightly.

His eyes gleamed in the reflected glow of the candlelight. They were a lion's eyes, she realized. Unblinkingly primal, laden with dangerous intent. "Come on, Abby, do I look like a man who'd use pretty phrases to get a woman into my bed?"

No, she determined, running her fingernail around the rim of her glass. That wouldn't be at all necessary. "I couldn't be less concerned with your lovemaking tactics."

He appeared honestly interested. "You haven't imagined us making love?"

"Not at all."

"I have."

She picked up her menu, pretending an extraordinary interest in the choice of appetizers. "I think I'll have the escargot," she decided. "They're excellent here. The sauce is loaded with garlic."

She peeked over the top of the menu, surprised to see the lambent desire in his eyes replaced by a patient smile. "Fine. So long as we both have them, it won't cause any problem when I kiss you."

"You won't be kissing me."

"Oh, yes, I will, Abby," Sam assured her. "Perhaps not tonight. But before all this is over. Trust me, you'll enjoy every minute." He lifted his glass in a slight toast.

She put the menu down and folded her arms on the tablecloth. "Are you always this self-confident?"

His tawny eyes lingered on her gleaming dark hair before moving onto her gray eyes, her slender nose, down to her full lips with a visual warmth that carried the impact of a physical caress.

"Are you always this lovely?"

His softly murmured words affected her far more than they should have. "Is this a pass?"

Those she knew how to deal with. It did disappoint her that Sam Garrett would behave in such a commonplace fashion when finding himself alone with Abby Swan/Jessica Thorne. For some reason, Abby had expected more from him. She thought, no, she'd *hoped* this man was different.

"It's not a pass."

She managed a light laugh. "That's funny, it sure looked like one to me."

He leaned closer, reaching across the table to cup her chin in his hand. "When I do make a pass, Abby, believe me, you'll recognize it."

Quite suddenly her lips went dry. "Hey you," she protested softly.

His thumb traced the outline of her upper lip. "Would it really kill you to call me Sam?"

Abby was an actress; she earned her living playing parts totally alien to her character and right now she was relying on all her talents to get her through the next few moments. He was good, she considered with reluctant admiration. Despite his sometimes arrogant behavior, Sam Garrett possessed a sensitivity that enabled him to pick up on the slightest nuance. She had the uneasy feeling that keeping anything from this man would be a full-time endeavor.

"Look," she began again, calmly, sensibly. "I'm not looking for an affair right now. My life is too hectic to establish any kind of relationship."

"I'm not looking for an affair, either," he assured her truthfully.

"Then we shouldn't have any problem."

"None at all," he agreed. While his tone was outwardly casual, his gleaming gold eyes and seductively husky voice conspired to hold her spellbound. "Of course, sometimes things happen when you least expect them."

Abby felt like flinging her arms around the tuxedoed waiter who suddenly appeared to take their order, interrupting this increasingly uncomfortable conversation. Before she could open her mouth, however, Sam proceeded to take the initiative.

"The lady will have the escargot appetizer, grilled Petaluma duck with lingonberry sauce, wild rice, asparagus, husk grilled corn and some of Rudolfo's excellent garlic bread," he ordered.

"Wait just one minute," Abby protested, annoyed at both his overbearing attitude and the amount of food he seemed to think her capable of consuming.

Sam ignored her spluttered complaint. "And a salad, but not your usual tossed green." He rubbed his chin thoughtfully. "Plum tomatoes should be good this time of year. And Bermuda onions, lightly seasoned with fresh herbs in a vinaigrette dressing. I'll have the same." He plucked the menu from Abby's fingertips, returning them both to the waiter, who gave a little half bow.

"Oh, and Black Forest cake for dessert," he tacked on, earning an incredulous stare from Abby.

"I hope Max'll give you a doggie bag," she stated dryly. "Because if you think I'm going to eat all that, you're crazy."

Her eyes flashed dangerously, but she kept her voice low in deference to the audience she knew she'd create if she shouted at him like she wanted to.

"It was not necessary to impress me with your ability to read a menu, Mr. Garrett. Besides, a gentleman always allows a lady a choice."

He braced his elbows on the table, linking his fingers together as he eyed her calmly across the intervening space. "I've never professed to be a gentleman, Abby. The sooner you understand that, the easier all this is going to be on both of us."

He half smiled, but there was no light in his amber eyes. "As far as ordering for you, it was necessary to establish the ground rules in this relationship."

"Ground rules?" she spat out suspiciously.

He nodded. "That's right. And rule number one is that I'm setting all the rules. Is that clear?"

"As mud," she muttered. "But it makes about as much sense as everything else about you."

"Have I piqued your curiosity about me, Abby?" he asked interestedly.

"Not about you," she corrected stiffly. "The only reason I'm here this evening is to hear this alleged plot to do me in that you and Jordan imagine you've uncovered."

"The only thing I've imagined about you, sweetheart, is how you'll feel in bed with me," he rasped. "That you are up to that lissome neck in danger is no idle threat. And I'm going to keep you out of trouble if I have to tie you up, lock you in a closet and throw away the key until we find the guy who's writing you those letters."

Abby flinched inwardly at the steel in his voice and took a long, calming drink of wine. "You *are* a dangerous man, aren't you, Mr. Garrett?" she murmured.

He shrugged off her softly issued question. "Perhaps dangerous times call for dangerous men."

There was a strength to Sam Garrett that surpassed any man she'd ever met. Her father had been a powerful, often ruthless man, but all his wars had been fought on corporate battlegrounds. She had the vague, uneasy feeling that Sam's battles had been far more primitively waged, with the stakes being lives, rather than stock certificates. At that idea, she recalled his limp and her mind whirled up any number of possible causes, each more disturbing than the rest.

Sam's intent gaze didn't miss Abby's slight shiver and he damned himself for putting it so harshly on the line. He'd gotten emotionally involved with this one, he realized, and was beginning to wish he'd never allowed Jordan Winston to talk him into it in the first place. But if he hadn't, Abby wouldn't be sitting across from him right now, the candlelight shimmering in her hair, making it gleam like ebony silk. She'd be dead. Crushed by that damn light yesterday.

"I'd never hurt you, Abby," he said gruffly. "You're going to have to trust me on that one."

The last lingering threads of irritation dissolved as Abby remembered that she owed this man her life. How on earth could she pay back such an enormous debt?

"I believe you," she said simply.

"Good." Sam smiled inwardly. Things were definitely looking up. "Truce?" he asked, lifting his glass in her direction.

"Truce," she agreed, raising her own glass in response before taking a sip of the smooth white wine.

She'd dropped her guard too soon, Abby realized. His eyes darkened, becoming like gleaming, molten gold.

"Want to try for friends?" he asked in a husky voice.

She took another sip of wine. "Aren't you rushing things, Mr. Garrett?"

"I thought we'd at least settled on 'hey you,'" he reminded her quietly.

Abby struggled against the pull of those dark eyes, that warm voice. *Dangerous,* she repeated to herself. *This man is definitely trouble.*

She opted for humor. "Hey you, aren't you rushing things?"

"Perhaps," he allowed. "But I think you need a friend right now, Abby."

"I have a lot of friends."

"I meant one you can trust."

She eyed him thoughtfully over the rim of her glass. He didn't appear to have any ulterior motive. "You really believe someone is trying to harm me, don't you?"

"I really believe someone is trying to kill you," he corrected.

Despite her lingering disbelief, a small tingling fear skittered up her spine. "Accidents do happen," she pointed out.

"Sure. But that light yesterday wasn't one of them. I'm not positive about your scuba diving mishap, but I know damn well the fire was arson."

"The fire department ruled it was an accident," she argued.

"That's because they don't know you."

"And you do?" she challenged.

"Enough to know that you're not the type of person to leave a burner set on high, then go to bed."

"I must have. There's no other explanation."

"There are a lot of other explanations," he countered. "And none of them are very pretty."

"Are you saying someone broke in and turned that burner on after I went to bed?" she asked incredulously.

"I'm saying that's a distinct possibility." He gave her a mock stern look. "Now I'm starving and would like to eat my dinner in peace. So why don't you shut up and eat? Then we'll discuss which, if any, of your boyfriends might have a motive to do you in."

Abby sucked in a harsh breath, but Sam appeared determined to ignore her rising anger as he picked up his fork and began to eat. Stifling a sigh, she began to pick at her own food, finding herself hungrier than she'd thought.

The escargot was as delicious as Abby remembered and she secretly admitted his choice in salad ingredients was inspired. She began to relax as they ate, and a little later, she stared in wonder at her empty plate.

How long had it been since she'd allowed herself to splurge like this? The role of Jessica Thorne was a demanding one and in order to fit into the woman's expensive wardrobe week after week, Abby usually ate little more than a dieting gerbil.

"You were hungry," Sam commented, glancing across the table at her empty plate.

"It was good," she allowed. "I can't remember the last time I ate so much at one meal."

"It sure couldn't hurt," he ventured, eyeing her wand-slim frame. It was still coming as a bit of a surprise that television's voluptuous Jessica Thorne was such a delicate woman.

"The cameras add about twenty pounds," she explained. "I have to watch my weight."

He shook his head. "Such are the sacrifices of art."

"Are you being sarcastic?"

Abby had learned to accept the fact that she did not earn her living with high drama. But it was good entertainment, and the ratings, which were viewed as gospel in the business, proved the series had developed a vast audience in this country and abroad.

"Are you being defensive again?" Sam countered.

"Perhaps," Abby admitted. She pushed aside her plate, bracing her elbows on the table, resting her chin on her linked fingers. "You know, the first four years I absolutely adored playing Jessica. She was so daring, so wonderfully decadent."

"And a far cry from the image Abby Swan presents to the world," he suggested softly.

She smiled at that. "You've very intuitive. I suppose that was part of the appeal. In the beginning."

"And now?"

"And now I'm getting a little tired of her," Abby admitted. "I really want . . ." Her voice drifted off.

"What do you want, Abby?" Sam asked quietly.

Abby didn't answer, not quite knowing how to explain to Sam that she wanted her own life. She'd been doing what others thought best for most of her nearly thirty years. It was time to think of her own needs, her own desires.

"Abby?" Sam repeated quietly.

She had a sudden need to escape his steady gaze. "Is it against the rules to go to the powder room?"

"I can't see where that would hurt," he allowed.

"Gee thanks," she responded with saccharine sweetness, rising from the table.

Once alone in the powder room, Abby dug through her purse, coming up with enough change to call Kenneth Swan from the pay phone hanging on the wall.

"Ken," she blurted out, casting nervous glances toward the door. She wouldn't put it past Sam to come barging in, if she was gone from the table too long. "Did you happen to discuss my letters with Jordan lately?"

"Not since he was in town for that fund-raising dinner," Kenneth replied. "What was that, two, three weeks ago?"

"About," Abby murmured thoughtfully.

"Abby?" Kenneth's voice held concern. "What's the problem? That guy hasn't written again, has he?"

"Uh-uh. But things took a weird twist today. Sam Garrett is from the FBI."

"What does he want with you?"

"He says he's just keeping an eye on me for Jordan, but he's been following me pretty closely. Ken, he knows about the beach house, the fire, everything."

There was a long silent pause on the other end of the phone. "You sure this guy is legit?"

"I saw his identification." She tried not to remember the gun she'd also seen strapped to Sam's hard body.

"ID's can be forged," Ken said thoughtfully. "Look, Abby, I'm going to check this guy out. Then I'll be right over."

"I'm not at home."

"Where are you? Not with him?" her brother asked incredulously.

"He took me to dinner."

Abby could practically see Ken raking his long, slender fingers through his blond hair as he sighed with exasperation.

"Take a cab home," he instructed tersely. "I'll meet you there."

"But Ken—"

"I want you to get the hell out of there, Abby. Now!"

Before she could argue further, the sound of Ken slamming the receiver down reverberated in her ear. Knowing her brother, Abby guessed he was probably halfway to Malibu already.

Deciding that he might have a point, Abby hung up the telephone. Their table was in an isolated corner of the restaurant; if she was careful, she could leave without Sam being any the wiser. Not that she wouldn't pay for that little act of rebellion later, but even if Sam Garrett was honestly working in her best interests, she was already tired of his overbearing attitude. It would do him good to discover she wasn't the pushover he'd obviously taken her for. Her heart was racing as she slipped out the door of the powder room.

"Going somewhere?" the unmistakable deep voice inquired.

Sighing heavily, Abby risked a glance upward at Sam, standing outside the door in the deserted hallway. Although his face was set in an expressionless mask, she couldn't miss the anger glittering in his eyes.

4

ALTHOUGH IT TOOK every bit of acting talent Abby possessed, she managed to meet Sam's intent gaze with a level one of her own.

"I'm suddenly very tired. I'd like to go home."

He inclined his head. "Fine. We can discuss this just as easily at your place, although you're probably going to break Rudolfo's heart. He's extremely proud of his Black Forest cake."

He cupped her elbow with a casual enough gesture, but his fingers were firm as he led her toward the front door of the restaurant.

"I can take a cab home, Mr. Garrett," she protested. "Malibu must be out of your way."

Sam clucked his tongue. "Abby, Abby," he said on a deep sigh, "when are you just going to accept that we're stuck with each other for the duration?"

She was saved from answering by the maître d', who looked up as they passed. "Was everything satisfactory?"

"Excellent, as usual, Max. Tell Rudolfo we're sorry to have to skip out before dessert, but a slight emergency has come up. Miss Swan will have to sample his specialty next time."

Max's face creased into a broad grin as he handed Sam a small white box with a flourish. "Two pieces of Black Forest cake, to go."

When Sam reached into a pocket, Max shook his head. "The cake is on the house; it's bad enough you insist on paying for your meal when you come here. Let me at least do this."

Sam nodded his acquiescence as he handed the box to Abby. "Thanks, Max. Have a good evening."

Max's eyes slid to Abby. "You, too," the maître d' offered, his tone unmistakable.

"You seem to be very popular," she commented as they drove up the Pacific Coast highway.

"Max and I go back a long way."

"Am I allowed to ask how you met?"

He gave her an assessing glance. "Curious about me, Abby?"

"Could you blame me if I was? After all, you seem to know everything about me, while I know little, if anything about you. I don't even know if you're married."

"Would it make a difference?"

"Of course not," she snapped, not quite truthfully. "I'd just like to even things up a bit, that's all."

The question of Sam's marital status had crossed her mind more than once during dinner, and Abby had decided that if FBI agents normally conducted their investigations in romantic, out-of-the-way restaurants, they must all be single, divorced, or leaving a lot of unhappy wives sitting at home.

"Max was being strong-armed by some people who wanted to take over his business," he revealed. "He didn't take it seriously at first, when they suggested he'd be happier using a certain linen supply company. Shortly after that, he was being told where to buy his produce, then his meat. By the time he called us, they were trying to buy him out."

"At some horribly deflated price," she guessed.

She watched his lips twist derisively. "Let's just say that they weren't offering fair market value."

Abby was interested, in spite of herself. "What happened?"

Sam lifted one broad shoulder in a careless shrug. "We'd had them under investigation for some time, but hadn't received any cooperation from the victims. Max agreed to tell them that I was his silent partner—the money man of the operation—and they'd have to deal with me."

Abby stared at Sam thoughtfully, wondering how he could state such facts so nonchalantly. "And?"

"I made a deal that brought me into the organization. Six months later, we had our indictments, Max had his business back, and there were a lot of happy restaurant owners in town."

"You went undercover as a gangster?" she asked incredulously.

"You've been watching too many Jimmy Cagney movies," he answered laconically. "They're called racketeers these days."

"Gangsters, racketeers, it was still dangerous." Once more Abby wondered if Sam Garrett was married. She knew, were the man her husband, she'd never get any sleep, wondering if that was the night he wasn't going to come home.

"I suppose it was," he agreed noncommittally.

"You could have been killed."

Sam didn't miss the slight tremor in her voice. Once again he eyed her with renewed interest. "Does that bother you, Abby? The idea of me being killed?"

Abby was surprised at just how distressful that thought was proving. It took a major effort to keep her tone casual.

"All this talk of killing is getting on my nerves. Could we change the subject, please?"

He shrugged again, but a slight smile played across his lips as Sam realized Abby was not as immune to him as she was pretending to be.

"Sure," he agreed easily. "Oh, and for the record, Abby, I'm not married."

If she had been worried before about her unwilling attraction to Sam Garrett, Abby was aghast at how that little bit of information lightened her heart.

Kenneth Swan's BMW was parked in Abby's driveway. As Sam and Abby exited their car, Ken was out of the BMW like a shot.

"You had me scared half to death," Ken exclaimed, sweeping Abby into his arms.

Abby patted her brother's cheek reassuringly. "As you can see, I'm fine."

Ken looked over Abby's shoulder. "I called the local FBI office, and when you hear what I discovered about your Mr. Garrett, you can understand why I was worried about you."

Abby watched the two men exchange a look that was anything but friendly. "Ken?" she asked, backing out of his arms, her glance moving from Sam's shuttered expression to her brother's antagonistic one. "What are you talking about? What do you know about Sam?"

As Abby's voice deepened on Sam's name, Ken's blue eyes pinned him with a particularly sagacious gaze. "You don't waste any time, do you?"

"You're talking about your sister," Sam reminded him softly.

"I'm well aware of that, Garrett," Ken ground out between clenched teeth. "Just as I'm aware of the fact that you've been lying to her from the beginning."

Sam was irritated by Kenneth Swan's arrival, having preferred to handle things in his own time and his own way.

Abby's half brother had managed to take that option away from him and he wasn't at all pleased.

"What?" Abby reached out, putting her hand on Ken's arm. She could feel the muscles tensing as his hand balled into a tight fist. "What are you talking about?"

"Did you call Jordan about this guy?" Ken asked her.

"I tried from the studio, but he was out."

"Look, Swan," Sam suggested, "why don't we continue this conversation somewhere else?"

"I don't think that's necessary," Ken stated brusquely, "since you're going to be leaving here in another minute."

"Would you please just get to the point," Abby instructed her brother firmly. "What has Mr. Garrett lied to me about?"

So, we're back to formalities, Sam considered angrily. He had a good mind to put his fist right into Kenneth Swan's face, wiping off that self-satisfied expression once and for all. It hadn't been easy to get Abby to lower her guard, and the guy had managed, in a few brief minutes, to undo what had taken him all evening to accomplish.

"He's not with the FBI, Abby."

"Damn it, now you've done it." Sam shot Ken a furious glare as Abby's gray eyes grew wide with unmasked fear and Sam was even more tempted to punch the guy out. His fingers curled over her shoulders as he held her at arm's length. "Look, Abby, I was going to tell you later—"

"Let go of her or you'll regret it," Ken stated icily.

Abby moaned softly and Sam smothered a harsh oath as they both viewed the revolver the man was pointing in Sam's direction.

"I hope, for your sake, that you've got a permit for that thing," Sam stated.

"Of course I do. Not that any legalities would prevent me from killing anyone who tried to harm my sister."

Abby had heard all she wanted to about killing for one day. "Would someone please tell me what's going on?"

Ken didn't remove his eyes from Sam as he kept the gun pointed directly at his chest. Sam inwardly cursed himself for leaving his own weapon in the car. He'd taken off the shoulder holster, knowing it had made Abby uneasy. Everything he'd learned about Kenneth Swan had indicated the man was not given to rash behavior. But experience had taught Sam never to count on anything when you had a gun trained on you.

"I checked the guy out," Ken told her. "It's true he used to work for the FBI, but he hasn't for the past nine months."

Sam mentally gave Abby points for self-control as she slowly turned her gaze toward him. "I'm sure Mr. Garrett has an explanation."

"I've taken a leave of absence," he answered simply.

"That's not good enough," Ken argued. Sam didn't like the rising fury he read in the man's blue eyes.

"I'll tell Abby everything she needs to know. After you've put that gun down."

"No way. How do we know you're not the lunatic who's been threatening her?"

Abby studied Sam's impassive expression carefully, deciding that while the man might be many disturbing things, he wasn't the unbalanced individual who'd been writing those letters.

"Ken," she requested, "please put it away. You're making me extremely nervous."

"Me?" He gave her an incredulous look. "It's Garrett you should be afraid of, Abby. Not me."

"I'm not afraid of you, Ken," she said softly, unnerved by the muscle jerking along her brother's jawline. She'd never seen him so angry. He seemed within an inch of losing control.

Sam came to the same conclusion and an eerie sense of déjà vu washed over him. The last time he'd seen that expression in a man's eyes, he'd been shot and left for dead on that remote Caribbean island. Not wanting to repeat the experience, he took advantage of Kenneth Swan's momentary inattention and lunged, knocking the revolver to the gravel underfoot.

"Don't try it," he advised, as the man's startled gaze cut from Abby, to Sam, to the revolver. "I'm not wild about having my life threatened, Swan. Push me a little bit more and you'll find out exactly how little it would take for me to lose my temper."

All the fight seemed to go out of Abby's half brother. His shoulders sagged. "What are you doing here?"

Sam didn't answer immediately. Keeping his eyes on the pair, he squatted down and picked up the revolver, emptying it before handing it back to Ken.

"I'm here as a favor to Jordan Winston," he said simply.

"But do you work for the FBI?" Abby asked, praying that she hadn't misjudged Sam.

"I'm still on payroll," he revealed. "I told you the truth, Abby, I'm on a temporary leave of absence. I got into a little trouble last year that landed me in the hospital. When I got out, I decided to take some time off." His amber eyes offered reassurance as he directed his gaze only to Abby. "I was packed and ready to go steelhead fishing in Idaho when Jordan came to me about those letters you'd been getting."

"That's why Jordan asked for the letters," she stated thoughtfully. "While I was glad to get rid of them, I couldn't figure out why he wanted them."

"Jordan turned them over to me so I could get the lab guys busy on tracing the stationery. I told you, it's a federal crime to send death threats through the mail, Abby. While in the beginning I wasn't convinced the guy was anything more than a frustrated fan who was more loosely wrapped than normal, he was still breaking the law. In the meantime, I promised Jordan I'd keep an eye on you, just in case."

"I suppose you can prove all that," Ken challenged.

Sam's eyes didn't leave Abby's. "I can. And I will."

"Abby, you can't trust this guy," Ken protested.

She chewed thoughtfully on a fingernail, studying Sam for a long, silent moment. Her eyes gave him the answer first. "I do," she said softly. Then she turned to her brother. "Ken, I really do appreciate your concern, but don't you think you should get back to Kristin?"

"I don't want to leave you alone with him."

"I'll be fine."

Ken thrust his fingers through his hair, obviously frustrated. "You're the most stubborn lady I've ever known."

She managed a smile at that. "Aren't you glad I am? You weren't the easiest man to locate."

He shook his head, returning her smile with a slight grin of his own. "I owe you a lot, Abby. And I love you. You know I just worry about you, kiddo."

Going up on her toes, she kissed his cheek. "I know all that. And I still can't get over my good luck to have such a terrific big brother to watch over me." She patted his arm. "But I can take care of myself on this one, Ken. Honest."

His blue eyes still held little seeds of doubt, but he expelled a soft sigh as he moved toward the BMW. Before getting into the car, he fixed Sam with a warning glare. "You do one thing to hurt her, Garrett, and you'll have to answer to me."

Sam nodded. "I'll remember that."

They remained silent, watching the BMW's taillights disappear. Then Sam and Abby stood in the center of the driveway, eyeing each other thoughtfully in the amber glow of her porch light.

"Did you call me Sam?"

She met his gaze with an even one of her own. "I guess I did."

"Does that mean we're friends?"

She shrugged carelessly. "I suppose anyone can always use a new friend."

He extended his hand toward her. "Want to shake on it?"

Again that slight lift of her shoulders as she held out her own hand. "Why not?"

His touch was more than she'd bargained for. The long fingers closing over hers were strong, his grip firm and not at all tentative. His thumb lightly stroked the tender skin at the inside of her wrist and she could only pray he hadn't felt the leap her pulse had just taken.

He had. "You're afraid again," he diagnosed softly, his eyes looking into hers, searching for hidden secrets.

Abby felt as if Sam was looking right into her soul. "No," she denied softly. "I'm not afraid." His thumb was still creating havoc with its light caress.

Sam smiled. "Good." He was in no hurry to let go of her hand. How could he be thinking of kissing her when there was so much at stake? His gaze surveyed her face, slowly, intimately.

"It's time for that talk," he stated finally.

Abby swallowed deeply, trying to escape the web of sensuality she could feel settling down around them. "I think you're right."

Despite her effort to appear unaffected by the moment of shared desire, Abby's hands gave her away by shaking as she tried to put her key in the lock. Sam took the key ring from her hand without comment, easily opening the weather-bleached door.

"I really like this place," he offered as they entered the living room, which looked out onto the vast expanse of blue

Pacific. "Despite the price tag, you've actually managed to make it homey."

Abby couldn't miss the unspoken accusation in his tone.

She glanced over at him, leaning against a wall, his arms folded over his chest. "That's the second implication that I should feel guilty about my money. Don't tell me you're a communist, Sam?"

He lifted a mocking brow. "A communist working for the FBI? Come on, Abby, give me a break."

"They've already discovered one agent who sold secrets to the Russians," she pointed out. "How do I know there aren't a few closet communists working there?"

"There may be, but I'm sure as hell not one of them."

"But you resent me because I grew up with that proverbial silver spoon in my mouth, right?"

Did he? Sam considered the question thoughtfully. He admittedly envied her this place, but he didn't resent her for being able to afford it, while he'd probably have to sock away his salary for the next year just to make one month's payment.

"I didn't mean for it to sound that way," he apologized. "It's none of my business where you choose to live, Abby." Sam decided to drop the subject before he ended up saying something he'd regret. "And I'm honestly glad the fire didn't go beyond the kitchen. It'd be a real shame to see all this go up in flames."

His roving gaze took in the blue and yellow floral sail-cloth cushions on the white wicker furniture, the art posters hung on the wall and the bright blue rug in the center of the white Mexican tile flooring. Green plants flourished in the moist sea air, giving an aura of tropical comfort to the casually decorated room.

"You didn't leave that burner on, Abby," Sam stated suddenly. "You're too levelheaded for that."

If she really hadn't done it . . . The idea was too outrageous for words. "Are you trying to scare me?" she asked quietly.

"Perhaps," he admitted. "But just enough so you'll listen to reason. This isn't some make-believe plot line from *Potomac*, Abby. This is real life, and I believe you're in danger. It's imperative you believe that, too."

Abby shook her head slowly, unable to quite accept his words. "No one would have any reason to kill me," she argued.

"Perhaps," he allowed. "But there's always the chance some lunatic out there thinks he's stalking Jessica Thorne."

Being as tired as she was, Abby found that thought too disturbing to handle right now. "Let's talk about your part in all this," she suggested softly.

Abby sat down on the couch, tucking her feet under her, watching with more than a little curiosity as Sam paced the room, obviously uncomfortable. She reminded herself that she had only Sam's word for what he was doing here. Was she mistaking sexual attraction for trust and friendship?

No. There had been more than desire in those tawny eyes. There had been honest concern. Sam Garrett was exactly the kind of man Jordan Winston would have for a friend, she considered. Strong, loyal and dependable. She smiled to herself, remembering how Jordan had called her only last week, asking what she wanted for her birthday. He'd called her Princess, the nickname he'd dubbed her with when she was toddling around in diapers and she'd laughed, telling him that if he ran across any Prince Charmings in Washington, she'd settle for one of her own.

To be honest, Abby mused, Sam was no Prince Charming. But he was undeniably the most intriguing man she'd ever met. Then she recalled his expression as he'd watched Ken leave. His eyes had glittered with a cold, dangerous light and she'd realized then Sam Garrett could also be ruthless. She'd have to remember that.

Sam stopped in front of the large window, his hands shoved into his back pockets as he stared out at the sea. A big white moon bathed the area, making the waters glisten like a shimmering sheet of silver. It was a night to talk of love, he considered, not killing. Sam hadn't wanted to tell Abby about his past. Not that he wasn't tempted, for personal reasons, to play on her sympathies. Hell, he was coming to the unwelcome realization that he'd be willing to do whatever it took to get Abby Swan into his bed.

But he forced himself to remember what had brought him here in the first place. Despite his initial reactions to Jordan's worries, Sam had come to the conclusion that someone was seriously stalking Abby, cunningly planning these little traps to make her death look like an accident. It was only her incredible luck that had kept her alive this far. And although he was a firm believer in luck, Sam knew it wouldn't continue to be enough. He needed more than Abby's trust; it was necessary that she understand he was the expert. The problem was, that little fiasco in the Caribbean didn't enhance his credibility very much.

He shook his head, turning around to face her. "My last assignment was working on a joint effort with the Justice Department's task force on drugs."

A small line of concern deepened her brow. "I've heard that can be very dangerous." What was it with Sam Garrett, Abby wondered. Did the man get some kinky thrill about putting his life on the line day after day?

He shrugged. "You get used to it," he stated. "I've known ordinary city cops to get blown away when they stop the wrong guy for going five miles over the speed limit. It comes with the territory."

"I suppose so," she murmured.

"My partner and I infiltrated a drug smuggling ring working out of Miami. I went down to the Caribbean to arrange a buy while Kyle stayed back in the states and arranged for the bust."

"Kyle was your partner?"

"Yeah." His tone was flat.

"He's dead, isn't he?" she asked, dreading the answer.

Sam rubbed his hand over his face. When he took it away, his amber eyes were devoid of any life. "Yeah. He'd found out we'd been made and was trying to get word to me when he got it."

"So you went ahead with the deal, never knowing what had happened?"

"That's about it. I still haven't figured out why they didn't just kill me in the hotel room. Instead, after they beat me up, they took me into the hills and shot me, leaving me for dead. I was lucky; some kids came along the next day and found me." He decided there was no point in describing the tortures that had gone on for three days before his captors had grown bored with their sadistic brand of fun.

"Lucky," she said softly. "How badly were you injured?"

"I spent eight months in the hospital" was all Sam offered for details. "Then I took some time off to decide if I wanted to spend the rest of my life behind a desk."

"You still have injuries?" Her eyes moved over his tall, hard frame. That was the reason for his limp, she decided, wondering if he was in pain right now and hating the idea.

"Nothing that will keep me from protecting you."

"I wasn't asking that, Sam. I want to know if you're still hurting."

He couldn't allow himself to respond to the gentle light in her eyes, so he lied. "No."

She gave him a soft smile. "I'm glad. . . . What do we do now?" she asked suddenly.

Entranced by her smile, Sam's mind had been indulging in a few fantasies when her question broke into his thoughts. It took him a moment to realize she was referring to his reason for being here with her.

"I've got a line on the stationery," he advised her. "We should know where it was purchased any time. As for now, I'd suggest we both get some sleep."

She nodded, wearily rubbing the back of her neck. Trying his best to ignore the way the gesture pulled the silky material of her scarlet blouse over her breasts, Sam dragged his gaze to her face.

Abby couldn't think with those eyes sweeping over her face, settling unnervingly on her lips. "That's a good idea," she agreed a little breathlessly.

"You've had a long day."

"So have you," she pointed out, slowly lowering the hand at her neck, appalled to discover it was trembling.

This is lunacy, he warned himself. The thing to do was turn around and leave the room now. "I'm used to it."

Abby folded her arms across her chest for protection. Her breasts were suddenly full and aching. "So am I."

This conversation was going nowhere. What was the matter with her? She was usually a witty conversationalist, but suddenly her brain had gone to mush, her words meaningless even to her own ears. Abby pushed herself up from the couch.

"Well, then, I guess it's time for you to go home," she suggested.

"I suppose I should," he agreed. But his feet seemed to be bolted to the floor and he heard himself saying things he'd meant to keep hidden in the furthermost reaches of his mind.

"You should always live at the beach, Abby. You and the sea have a great deal in common."

Her eyes softened as their gazes met, silver meeting gold. "What do you mean?" she asked quietly.

"You appear so calm, so serene, yet you have hidden depths. You can turn stormy at a moment's notice and your voice . . . Ah, Abby, your lush voice is so seductive, so inviting, that any man would willingly drown in your arms."

His murmured words, as well as his gleaming, hypnotic eyes wrapped Abby in a silken web and she remained frozen where she stood, staring up at his roughly hewn face. The room was bathed in a white, misty glow and Abby knew that if she didn't break this sensuous spell soon, it would be too late.

She jerked away, going to the window where she wrapped her arms around herself, as if for protection. She had turned her back to Sam as she gazed unseeingly out the wide expanse of glass.

"You're very poetic for an FBI agent," she said finally in what she hoped was a light tone. "I had no idea a man in your field could write such good dialogue."

"I had an excellent muse," he said simply. "I can't believe you haven't inspired men to poetic thoughts before."

"Not really. Usually their fantasies are a bit more earthy."

"Oh, I'll admit to a few of those myself, sweetheart," he said huskily.

It was then she made the mistake of turning around. Abby warned herself not to be affected by his sensuous smile. She knew it was time to go to bed, but she couldn't make herself leave this room. Not while his darkening eyes were so effectively holding her hostage.

"Abby."

His deep tones rolled over her name, caressing it, and Abby thought she'd never heard it sound so wonderful. As if in a trance, she drew closer, stopping a few inches from him.

"What?" she whispered.

Sam's eyes slid down her taut frame, detecting the trembling of her slender body as she awaited his next move. He closed his eyes and expelled a slight, almost regretful sigh. As Abby watched, he shook his head, as if fighting this shared moment of intimacy.

Then his eyes suddenly opened, colliding with hers, the message raw and unmistakable. "Just . . . Abby," he said, moving to within a whisper of her body.

She could feel the warmth his body generated and unable to resist, she reached out, tentatively pressing her palm against the front of his shirt.

"This is insane," she murmured.

Sam covered her hand with his, increasing its pressure, letting her feel the harsh beat of his heart. "Sheer lunacy," he agreed.

"I don't even know you," she protested softly, doing nothing to stop him as he drew her slowly into his arms.

Sam buried his lips in the fragrant silkiness of her hair, trying to achieve some control over the desire running rampant through him. If he had an ounce of common sense, he'd leave right now. He had no business touching her. He shouldn't want her. He had enough trouble in his life at the moment, he didn't need to complicate things by taking Abby to bed. He warned himself to get out while he still could. To keep his distance. But even as Sam told himself all that, his body overruled his mind and he pulled her even closer.

"All you need to know is how right we are for each other," he responded gruffly. "How good we'll be together."

He made it sound so simple. But Abby knew there was nothing simple about Sam Garrett. He'd accused her of having hidden depths, but every instinct she possessed told her that his went far deeper. Every time she'd attempted to get close, tried to learn something concrete about him, he'd smoothly backed away, erecting a steel barricade between them. Involvement with such a man, Abby told herself firmly, could only lead to heartbreak.

She couldn't help stiffening at that idea, just as she couldn't stop Sam from feeling her instinctive response. "No," he murmured, his arms tightening around her, denying her the opportunity to pull away. "Not yet."

Abby's heart fluttered against her ribs as Sam fit her deliciously into the cradle of his thighs. They were as close as two individuals could be without the total intimacy of consummation. When she breathed, she felt the answering movement of his chest. When she sighed, she felt his own warm breath fanning her hair. And as his hand pressed against the small of her back, fitting her to his stirring virility, Abby experienced a respondent warm ache flooding throughout her lower body. Her own hands moved up his chest, across the hard line of his shoulders, banishing the last barrier between them as her fingers linked together around his neck.

Sam's eyes turned to molten gold as they roamed her uplifted face, settling on her mouth. "Insane," he murmured. Every nerve ending in Abby's body was poised, ready for the kiss she knew was coming. Overwhelmed by the passion glowing in his eyes, her own lids fluttered closed.

It would be so easy, Sam mused. Abby had been under a great deal of stress the past few months. His presence in her life had increased that pressure, and he knew the scene with her half brother had disturbed her deeply. She was unnerved and incredibly vulnerable. With an intuitive male sense, Sam knew that with the slightest effort, he could spend the night making love to the delectable Abby Swan. Just as he knew he couldn't do it. Too much depended on her trusting him and seducing her in a weak moment was no way to forge a relationship.

The light peck on her forehead came as both a surprise and a disappointment. Abby's eyes flew open, raking over his face, but he'd donned that expressionless, professional mask that made her want to scream.

"I'll see you tomorrow morning," he said smoothly, as if the seductive scene they'd shared was only a fleeting fantasy.

Abby pulled away, fixing him with a pair of gray eyes that had hardened to cold steel. "I'm busy tomorrow morning."

"You're meeting with the banker," he agreed, nodding his head. "I'm going along."

Still shaken by the desire that had whipped through her, Abby welcomed the rush of irritation caused by his imperious tone. Her hands curled into fists at her hips.

"The hell you are, Sam Garrett! I have enough at stake without you blowing it for me."

"I'll be so inconspicuous you won't even notice me," he promised.

"You're not coming with me," she repeated firmly. There was silence from Sam. "Well?" she prompted a response.

"I'll see you in the morning," he stated abruptly, turning on his heel to leave. "Don't forget to lock this door," he instructed.

"I was going to," she snapped, nevertheless following him.

He turned in the doorway, placing a finger under her chin, lifting her smoldering gaze to his. "Don't fight it, Abby. You're stuck with me, like it or not. Now you can make the experience sheer hell for both of us by fighting me at every turn, or you can relax a little and let me do my job."

"When you suggest I relax," she stated brusquely, "I suppose that includes going to bed with you?"

"I want you, Abby," Sam said, suddenly serious. "Far more than I ever believed possible, far more than I should. But no, I don't need you in my bed to keep an eye on you. That would only be a pleasant bonus."

His head swooped down, planting a quick, possessive kiss against her lips that left her tender skin tingling. Then before Abby had time to recover from the surprise, he was gone. So intent was she on watching Sam's taillights disappear down the highway, she failed to notice the darkened car parked across the street.

5

IN WHAT WAS BECOMING a disconcerting habit, Sam once again found sleep an elusive target as he lay on his back, his head pillowed by his arms, his mind filled with thoughts of Abby Swan.

He'd learned a lot about Abby from Jordan Winston. Some digging had provided more facts, but that's all they were. Facts. Hard, cold, unemotional data that appeared to tell him everything while revealing nothing. He knew how tall she was. Five feet, four inches tall. An ordinary enough height, but he knew Abby to be far from ordinary. She weighed a slender one hundred and three pounds, but every ounce contributed to a body that invited a man's most erotic fantasies.

Her driver's license reported her hair to be black, her eyes gray. Nowhere did it mention that the thick dark waves cascading over her shoulders were ebony silk, or that her wide eyes sparkled silver with emotion and were fringed with thick, curly black lashes. And her voice, that husky, marvelous voice, could kindle fires in the coldest of men.

She was like no one he'd ever met, and as Sam lay staring up at the ceiling, he realized that not only did Abby surpass all previous women of his acquaintance, but the odds of ever meeting anyone again remotely as desirable as Abby Swan were nil.

He couldn't imagine anyone wanting to harm her, let alone kill her. But he firmly believed someone out there was giving it his best shot and all past assignments paled in significance to keeping Abby safe. Keeping her alive. The problem was, right now he was working in the dark. He could only hope tomorrow would bring some pertinent information. If not . . .

That unpleasant thought kept Sam awake late into the night.

As ABBY RETRIEVED her newspaper from the driveway the next morning, she had the uneasy sensation she was being watched. Warily lifting her gaze, she saw Sam, sitting in his car across the street. Shaking her head, she went over to him.

"Did you sit out here all night?" she asked incredulously.

"No, a friend of mine pulled night duty. I've only been here a couple hours."

Some quick calculations told Abby that Sam couldn't have had more than five hours' sleep. "Aren't you exhausted?"

"I've gotten by on a lot less sleep than this," he said, brushing off her concern.

"Watch that tough guy act, Sam," she advised lightly. "You're in danger of becoming a stereotype." Then she smiled. "Since I have the strong feeling that you're not going to go away, you may as well come in for a cup of coffee."

He opened the car door. "I've received more gracious invitations from ladies in the morning, but these days I suppose I'll have to take what I can get." Sam forced a wry smile, trying not to grimace as he put his weight down onto his aching leg, but Abby didn't miss the fleeting shadow of pain that crossed his face.

"Oh, here," he said, reaching into the front seat to take out the white bakery box. "With all the excitement your brother caused last night, we forgot Rudolfo's Black Forest cake. How would you like to be really decadent and have it for breakfast?"

"I don't eat breakfast."

"You should, you know," he argued conversationally. "It's—"

"I know," Abby interjected, "the most important meal of the day. But I still detest eating anything before noon."

Sam looked inclined to argue further, but decided against it.

"Have you taken anything for that?" she asked as they walked back to the house. She noticed Sam was doing his macho best not to limp, but his gait was stiffer than yesterday.

"Can't," he muttered. "Pain pills make me too groggy."

"Oh. Does it hurt all the time?"

Sam didn't like talking about his leg. It made him feel like a damn invalid. Wasn't it enough it had forced his retirement from field work? Pity was one emotion he didn't want to view in Abby Swan's gentle eyes.

"No. It's just a little stiff from being cramped up in the car in this moist ocean air. Don't worry about it," he advised gruffly.

Abby knew better than to push. She remained silent as they entered the house, Sam following her into the kitchen.

"They did a good job," he commented, his amber gaze circling the cheery room.

"Didn't they," she agreed, putting the box down on the counter as she took a ceramic mug from a copper rack. "Black, no sugar, right?"

"You remembered."

He sounded inordinately pleased and Abby knew that to allow herself to respond to the self-satisfaction in his tone would only be asking for trouble. "It was only last night," she pointed out stiffly, refusing to look at him as she poured the steaming coffee.

"I know. But I can't get over the feeling that I've known you all my life," he replied, as Abby brought the mug over to the table.

Realizing belatedly that it was a foolhardy thing to do, she made the mistake of meeting his suddenly intent gaze. The hunger in his amber eyes reached out to her, surrounding her in a gleaming gold web of desire.

Unable to resist touching her, Sam reached out, his hands splayed against the back of her thighs as he pulled her a little nearer. "I lied."

Abby's lips were suddenly very dry, but as she licked them with the tip of her tongue, she knew she'd made another tactical error. The hunger flared in Sam's eyes. "Lied?" she whispered.

"Lied. I didn't get any sleep at all last night, Abby. I couldn't get you out of my mind. I kept thinking of how it was going to be when we made love. I could feel your slender, responsive body lying beside me; I could taste the sweet honey of your lips, your skin; I imagined how it would feel to have you take me deep inside you, making us one. . . ."

His stroking fingers were creating havoc on the back of her legs, and Abby felt as if Sam had hypnotized her with those blazing golden eyes.

"What do you think about when you imagine us making love, Abby?"

"I don't," she lied in a shaky voice.

He took her free hand and placed it on his chest. "Touch me and tell me that."

Abby could feel the warmth of his body through the crisp white shirt. The steady beat of his heart thudded with increased vigor against her fingertips, and for a moment she was entranced, realizing it was synchronized with her own heartbeat. She was suddenly swept with an urge to explore this phenomenon further, and reached blindly for the table, planning on putting down the near forgotten coffee mug so she could unbutton his shirt and experience the smoldering warmth of his skin firsthand.

"Oh, no!" Abby cried out as the cup went crashing to the tile floor and Sam was out of the chair in a shot, barely missing having coffee splattered all over his gray suit. Abby stared at the mess she'd made, aghast at her uncharacteristic clumsiness.

"Got a mop?" Sam asked casually.

Abby was still staring at the spreading dark stain. "In the broom closet," she mumbled, waving her arm absently in that direction.

"No sweat." Before she could open her mouth to object, Sam was busy mopping up the spilled coffee.

"I can do that," she protested. "You're going to get your suit messy."

He shrugged. "Hey, I'm an expert at this. I put myself through college messing for a sorority at UCLA, so I'm used to cleaning up after klutzy, beautiful women."

Despite her discomfort watching him mop her floor while dressed in that serious gray suit, Abby realized that Sam had just offered a tidbit of information about himself. Latching onto it, she tried for more. "You went to UCLA?"

Satisfied that he'd gotten the last of the dark liquid, he rinsed the mop out in the sink. "Yeah."

"I went to USC."

"That figures." He opened the kitchen door, putting the mop outside to air.

His back had been turned toward her and Abby thought she'd detected a slight sarcasm in his muffled response. "What figures?"

Sam didn't answer as he poured himself another cup of coffee. "Want a refill?"

"Thanks," she responded absently, handing him her own mug. "Sam, what figures?" she pressed again.

When he handed her the coffee, his eyes were shielded, his face expressionless. "It figures that you went to USC. I can't see Matthew Swan's daughter mingling with the plebian crowd found at a public university."

"You know," she advised softly, eyeing him over the rim of the mug, "I'm surprised that your shoulder doesn't give you a great deal more discomfort than your leg."

"Why?" he asked suspiciously, his eyes narrowing.

"That's some gigantic chip you're carrying around. It must be very heavy."

Sam grimaced, knowing that he was wearing his prejudices on his sleeve again. "Touché. I apologize for my less-than-gallant statement."

Abby observed him thoughtfully, her irritation dissolving as she watched the rueful expression flicker in his eyes. "And I apologize for my clumsiness." She sighed. "I'm not my best in the morning."

Sam rubbed his chin as he submitted her to a longer, more thorough study. She was dressed in a white eyelet robe that belted at the waist, outlining her slender curves as it fell to the floor. He watched the rise and fall of her breasts under the delicate material and it occurred to Sam that the combination of the modest, almost virginal robe and the smoky sexuality in Abby's gray eyes were an intriguing mix. God, how he wanted her.

"I'd have to argue with that," he stated finally, his eyes darkening as they moved across her face.

Unsettled by the desire in his eyes, Abby sought to escape the seductive spell he'd woven around them once again. "Honestly," she said, "I am definitely not a morning person. I can't think straight until I get my morning jolt of caffeine." She forced a perky grin. "It'd be terrific if I could figure out a way to take the stuff intravenously." She heard herself beginning to babble and cringed.

"You could always snort instant."

"That's a thought," she agreed.

Then another idea occurred to her. There was something Abby wanted him to understand, in case he had any preconceived notions about her. She was all too familiar with the unattractive stereotypes her profession garnered.

"I don't do drugs."

He turned a chair around, straddling it, his arms braced along the top. "I know," he said simply, taking a drink of coffee.

She wasn't that surprised. "You've done your homework very well," she murmured.

"It's my job," he reminded her. "If you were involved in the drug scene out here, Abby, it would be important for me to know it. That's a dangerous pastime."

His mouth tightened into a hard line, reminding Abby of just how dangerous Sam had already found the illegal drug business. He could have died, she reflected, realizing that if he had, she'd have never met him.

"What happened to you in the Caribbean, Sam?" she asked quietly.

Unwilling to discuss what he was still considering a failure, Sam rose from the table, rinsing out his mug. "If you're going to be on time for that meeting," he advised her casually, his gaze revealing nothing as he eyed her over his shoulder, "you should probably get dressed."

Frustrated by his retreating behind those well-developed parapets, Abby was on her feet immediately, slamming her own mug into the sink with a force that could have chipped the enamel, but didn't. Then, without a word, she walked stiffly from the room.

Heaving a deep sigh, Sam stared out the window at the veil of fog that was still wrapping itself about the beach house. It was a good morning for a fire. Knowing it was an exercise in masochism, Sam allowed himself the fantasy of lying with Abby in front of a fragrant cedar blaze, forgetting the harsh world that lay outside the beach house for a time while they explored the passion to be found in each other's arms.

Then, with brutal self-honesty, he reminded himself that he was supposed to be protecting Abby Swan. He couldn't allow his professionalism to be endangered by his desire for the woman. He paced the floor, forcing himself to refrain from going upstairs and ripping that demure white robe from her body to discover the steaming sensuality he knew lay hidden beneath her cool, composed exterior.

"I'm sorry," Abby said the moment she returned to the kitchen. "I didn't mean to pry into your private life, Sam."

He shrugged. "Don't worry about it." His amber eyes made a slow study of her appearance. "You look terrific."

She ran her palms over nonexistent wrinkles on the skirt of her raw silk ivory suit. "You don't think I look too soft?"

He arched an eyebrow. "Soft?"

Her fingers were trembling ever so slightly. "You know, too feminine?"

"I don't think you could look anything but," he answered honestly. "But if you're worried about not looking professional enough, don't bother. While that silky little suit is a far cry from gray serge, you don't look anything like Jessica Thorne, either."

She slanted him a crooked, appreciative smile. "I'll admit this meeting has me worried."

"You still haven't gotten the funding for *Medicine Woman*?"

Abby wasn't as surprised as she might have been two days ago that Sam knew about the film she wanted to do so badly. "It's not easy for a woman to be taken seriously in this business," she allowed. "We make pretty enough set decorations, but as far as handing over any control . . ."

She sighed, shaking her head. "I suppose you're still planning on coming with me," she stated flatly.

"That's the game plan."

"Well, let's go. And today I'd like to take my car."

"Something wrong with mine?" he inquired dryly.

"Nothing washing it wouldn't cure. But my father taught me a long time ago that the best way to get money was to look as if you don't need it."

He tried not to be offended by the fact that his three-year-old sedan hardly fit Abby's criteria. She was right of course. Image was everything in this town built on fantasy and illusion.

"You've succeeded admirably," he said blandly, taking in the demure strand of pearls that he knew were not simulated. Oil and water, he considered. That's what he and Abby were. Shake well and they might come together for a short time, but they'd never mix.

"Speaking of that," Sam asked as they left the house, "why don't you just fund the film yourself?"

She opened the driver's door of her Mercedes roadster. "It's a long story."

"We've got lots of time," he invited as he folded his tall frame into the compact car.

She inserted the key into the ignition, turning toward him before starting the engine. "Maybe later," she murmured.

That was enough for now. He nodded, remaining silent as she drove into downtown L.A., pulling into the parking garage of a large pink art deco building surrounded by towering mirrored high rises. Her stride was purposeful as she entered the building, and although Sam knew she was playing the role of a woman executive, the looks on the men's faces as she passed did not display interest in her financial statement.

Only when she pushed the button on the elevator did her nervousness manifest itself again. Her hands were shaking. Sam reached out, linking their fingers together, noticing how perfectly her hand fit in his. When she looked up at him, surprised by his action, he smiled.

"You'll be great," Sam said simply, squeezing her fingers. "They'll probably open their vaults and beg you to take whatever you want."

His amber eyes were quietly assuring as they smiled down at her and Abby realized that she was secretly grateful he was there to lean on. He was so sure of himself, so strong. So dangerous, she reminded herself. She couldn't allow herself to succumb to even a momentary weakness when she was around him. He saw too much with those steady, shrewd eyes.

Pulling her hand free, Abby dragged her gaze away, staring at the numbers flashing above the door. After an agonizingly long time the steel doors opened and she walked briskly down the hallway, Sam following silently behind.

She looked up at him, her hand on the knob of the frosted glass door. "Sam, you wouldn't—"

"I'll stay in the reception area, keeping my fingers crossed for you," he answered her unstated question.

She managed a weak smile. "Thanks."

He returned the smile with a brilliant, encouraging one of his own. "Go get 'em, Tiger."

As they entered the suite of offices, Abby experienced a sudden burst of possessiveness as the blond receptionist's liquid dark eyes drank in Sam as if she'd never seen a man before. Biting down her irritation, she gave her name to the woman, then settled stiffly on the edge of the leather couch, waiting to be admitted to the banker's inner sanctum.

When Sam continued to be an object of extreme interest, Abby cleared her throat. The young woman's gaze moved reluctantly toward her and Abby's gray eyes hardened, giving the receptionist an unmistakable message.

Mine, they professed, even as Abby secretly admitted she had no right. Sam was idly flipping through a copy of *Sports Illustrated*, outwardly oblivious to the silent duel between the two women. Finally the strident buzzer sounded on the woman's desk and she waved Abby toward the door behind her, blatantly pleased to be rid of the competition.

Once inside the banker's private office, Abby was forced to sit quietly while James Palmer, vice president in charge of commercial loans, examined her file, not saying a word. Every so often an iron gray brow would arch inquisitively, or dive down toward his Roman nose, but although he'd been reading the data she'd brought him for almost thirty minutes, the man had not commented on a single item. The absent tapping of the gold fountain pen on his desk blotter was driving her crazy.

He'd appeared interested while she had explained the project, Abby assured herself. She'd presented her case clearly and intelligently, stressing the financial benefits offered by *Medicine Woman*, not the artistic challenge she so longed for. She kept her hands folded calmly in her lap, wondering at the ability of an ice cold hand to perspire.

Finally the banker cleared his throat, causing Abby to lean forward in the leather chair. "This is all very interesting, Ms Swan," he allowed. "I can see that you've done your homework."

"Thank you." Did that mean he was agreeable? Had she gotten the funds?

"By the way," he added, "my wife and I never miss *Potomac*. We're both big fans of yours."

"Thank you," she repeated, wishing the man would just get to the point.

"Yes . . . Well." He cleared his throat again, then took off his reading glasses, folding the stems absently as he studied her. "It's a compelling synopsis; I can see it doing very well at the box office."

"The book won a Pulitzer Prize for fiction," she pointed out, allowing herself a glimmer of hope.

"I remember." He put down the glasses and began shuffling the papers uncomfortably.

Here it comes, Abby groaned inwardly, awaiting the words she'd heard far too many times the past two years. She didn't have to wait long.

"Have you considered optioning the property to someone else?"

"Someone else?" she asked innocently, lifting a dark brow.

"Yes. Someone with a bit more experience, a track record for achieving production success."

He was more subtle than most of the money men she'd encountered, but Abby suspected that was because a large share of Swan Pharmaceuticals was filtered through this man's bank.

"A man," she helped him out.

To his credit, the banker appeared uncomfortable. A red flush appeared above his collar. "Well, I know of few women who'd fit that criterion," he admitted.

"So," Abby stated briskly, "unless I'm willing to hand control over to someone else, I'm out of luck."

"It's a risky business, Ms Swan."

"I'm well aware of that, Mr. Palmer. But I know what I'm doing. I've worked with some of the best minds in the business; I've studied, I've even directed some of the episodes of *Potomac.*"

"Yes, all that was in your proposal. But you've never produced."

She leaned forward in her chair, her eyes intense as she tried to make her point. "Let me see if I understand this. I can't get backing to produce unless I've already produced, which I can't do unless I receive backing. Is that it?"

He looked as if she'd just discovered the secret of relativity, single-handedly. "Precisely."

Frustrated beyond belief, Abby was on her feet. "That's the stupidest bit of logic I've ever heard," she stated harshly. "It's a damn catch twenty-two and you know it!"

He only shrugged, gathering the papers together to return them to the file. She watched, seething with anger, as he lined up all the edges with the precision of a NATO field commander preparing for inspection.

"Thank you for your time," she said through gritted teeth, turning on her heel.

"Ms Swan?"

Abby turned in the doorway. "Yes?"

"There *is* one possible solution."

She felt her knees weakening. Perhaps she still had a chance. Damning her unruly tongue, Abby forced her expression into a casual one. "What are you suggesting?"

"You could always put up some Swan Pharmaceuticals stock for collateral."

"Perhaps you've forgotten, Mr. Palmer, I don't have sole control over my father's company. There is a board of directors to consider."

"And you're chairman of the board," he reminded her. "Plus, in three weeks you'll be in a position to make such executive decisions on your own."

Abby nodded, knowing that if she forced the issue, she could easily sway the board. But she had no intention of funding the film with her father's money.

"I'll give that idea some thought," she murmured non-committally.

The banker nodded. "Why don't you do that, Ms Swan?" he agreed politely. "Let me know when you've come to a decision."

"I certainly will," she said with a cool smile, still playing the game. It took all her willpower not to slam the door as she left.

Sam put down the magazine the instant she entered the waiting room. Her flashing eyes told the story and refraining from commenting in front of the interested receptionist, he simply opened the door for her, easily keeping up with her long stride as she marched down the hall toward the elevator.

"Want to talk about it?" he inquired finally, as they exited the building.

"No."

"Okay," he agreed easily. "Want me to drive?"

Abby considered that offer for a moment, then handed him the keys. The mood she was in, she'd probably end up running over someone before they got back to the house.

"I've always wanted to drive a car like this," he remarked with a smile as he pulled the roadster out of the parking lot.

Abby remained silent, her blistering gaze directed through the windshield. Giving up on conversation for the time being, Sam maneuvered the car through the traffic, heading out of the heart of the city.

"I need to talk to you," Sam stated as he pulled the car into the garage. "Want to take a walk on the beach?"

She looked down at her silk suit. "In this?"

"I think you look absolutely lovely," he said, smiling down at her. "But you're right. It's not really appropriate beach attire. We'll change first, then talk."

"We?" she asked, casting a suspicious eye over his suit.

"I threw a few things into my car before I drove out here this morning," Sam admitted almost sheepishly.

Abby folded her arms across her chest. "Pretty sure of yourself, aren't you, Sam?"

"Not really," he answered, unfolding his tall frame from the low-slung car. "Are you going to sit in here all day?"

"One of these times, you're going to push too far," she muttered. "You can't always get everything you want."

Ain't that the truth, Sam considered, as they entered the sun-filled beach house. He remembered the year his father had died. The younger Garretts hadn't understood that their lives had altered drastically, although Sam, being the oldest, at twelve, knew his childhood days had come to an end. Jennifer and Jamie had worked for a week on their Christmas list and he hadn't missed the worried frown carving deeper and deeper lines on his mother's forehead as she'd watched the list grow. "You can't always get everything you want," she'd warned them.

Between them, Sam and Laura Garrett had tried; he'd contributed his paper route money, as well as the extra funds earned mowing lawns and doing odd jobs, to the scant amount Laura made as a housekeeper in one of those large mansions John Garrett had always promised would be hers someday. But most of the money went for necessities—rent, utilities and food—and since Laura's presence had been required to oversee the festive Christmas dinner of her employer, it had fallen upon Sam's shoulders to explain that even Santa could have a bad year.

Abby watched Sam's jaw harden as his eyes grew cold and distant. She followed his gaze out the window to the vast expanse of whitecapped surf, but could find nothing there to generate whatever dark thoughts he was obviously having. He continued to ignore her presence as she crossed the room to him.

"Sam?" she asked softly. "Is something wrong?"

He kept his eyes glued to the far horizon, knowing what he'd find if he looked down into Abby's face. Those soft gray eyes held a certain peril he couldn't allow.

"It's nothing," he assured her brusquely, turning away from the wall of glass. His eyes flicked with outward disinterest over her slender frame. "I thought you were going to change your clothes."

She ignored the pointed hint. "Are you certain you're all right? Your leg," she remembered belatedly, "are you in pain?"

Her soft touch on his arm affected him like a searing brand, and he jerked away. "I told you to forget any damn injuries I might have," he growled.

Abby stared up at him, momentarily stunned. "I just thought—"

"Damn it, you're not supposed to think," he interrupted harshly. "I do the thinking and you do what you're told."

"I'm sorry," she countered with cool restraint, ignoring the pain caused by his blistering dark gaze. "I hadn't realized that a little human kindness was against the rules."

Her words were ground out through clenched teeth, her back was as stiff as cold steel, but the hurt mirrored in her gray eyes gave her away. While Sam could take all the anger Abby could dish out, he was finding himself defenseless against her gentle sensitivity. He couldn't allow her to do this to him; he couldn't fall prey to her tenderness.

Hating himself, Sam glared down at her, tapping his finger against the face of his watch. "You have exactly five minutes to change your clothes and meet me outside."

"What makes you think I can change that fast?"

His expression was more intimidating than any she'd ever seen, but Abby relied on her store of talent to resist showing her nervousness as he leaned toward her. They were standing toe to toe, his eyes glittering dangerously as he lowered his head, his face inches from her own.

"In the first place, as an actress, you should be used to quick changes," he pointed out correctly. "And in the second place, I guarantee, sweetheart, if you leave the job to me, it'll take a helluva lot less than five minutes to strip those clothes off you."

"You can be a real bastard when you want to be, Sam Garrett," Abby observed quietly.

"Just keep that in mind," he warned, refusing to allow her to see how much that softly issued accusation hurt.

She surprised him by smiling sweetly. "Oh, I will," she promised. "Especially the next time someone's pointing a gun at you. I'll advise against aiming for your heart. Because you don't have one." She flounced from the room, marching briskly up the stairs, once again slamming her bedroom door behind her. The sound reverberated throughout the house.

Sam swore aloud, then followed to the second bedroom, changing out of the stifling suit into a comfortable pair of jeans and a blue polo shirt. Glaring at her still-closed door, he stomped downstairs and went outside.

6

As Abby changed her clothes, she reminded herself that she was nothing but an assignment Sam had taken on for an old friend. Well, she admitted, carefully hanging up her suit, there was a bit more going on under the surface. But was that really so unusual? Sam was an extremely virile man and the idea that he wanted her was undeniably exciting. Taking in the fact that she normally only dated men who could be charitably described as "safe," it was inevitable that she'd be experiencing these odd feelings of attraction.

That's all it was, Abby assured herself. Chemistry. An adolescent sexual fantasy for a man who represented more than his share of danger. Mindful of Sam's deadline, Abby finished dressing and met him on the beach under the wire.

"Well? Am I on time?"

Sam's amber eyes surveyed the faded jeans that fit her like a well-worn glove and the rainbow-hued gauze blouse that fell to her knees. She appeared younger than her thirty years, and a great deal more vulnerable than her screen image. He wondered what her legion of fans would think if they could see her now.

He grunted a positive response.

Refusing to be put off by his ill humor, Abby shrugged and breathed in the fresh sea air. The tangy salt scent went straight to her head, clearing away the distressing little cobwebs left by her distasteful encounter with James Palmer.

"Mmm," she sighed happily. "This was a perfect idea, Sam. How did you ever think of it?"

"It wasn't that difficult. You were upset, and I've always had the theory that taking some time to walk along the beach is pretty good therapy. When you're faced with that enormous expanse of Pacific Ocean, troubles don't seem nearly so big."

"That's how I've always felt," she admitted.

"I know."

"Now you're a mind reader?"

"Not really." He looked over at her for a long unsettling moment. "I'm a house reader."

Her arched brow invited him to elaborate. "If you didn't thrive on the sea, you wouldn't put up with all the hassles a beach house entails," he explained. "The flooding, the damp air, the salt corrosion. Besides, that beach house reminds me of you, Abby. Natural and unpretentious." He allowed a crooked smile. "If you ignore the price tag."

"You're too preoccupied with money, Sam." Abby's tone was gently accusing.

He could have answered that he was too preoccupied with *her* money. And his lack of it. But Sam decided that would open up a topic he wasn't prepared to discuss right now.

When he didn't answer her softly chiding statement, Abby sighed, and looked out over the expanse of blue water. Experience had taught her that far too many men were as much attracted by her family fortune as they were by her. But, if anything, Sam seemed to resent her wealth. Abby wondered why she was finding that so disturbing.

"Which way?" he asked suddenly, breaking into her worried thoughts.

Abby pointed up the beach. "That way. There's a little old man who's been at the same spot every day for years. He sells the best hot dogs you've ever tasted."

Sam arched a dark brow. "Hot dogs?"

"With onions," she agreed cheerfully. "Louie's chili dogs are my favorite thing in the entire world."

"Of course," he murmured dryly, "everyone knows chili dogs are the only food to serve with Dom Perignon."

Abby stopped short, her eyes displaying her hurt as she looked up at him. "How much money would I have to give away before you liked me, Sam?"

He jammed his hands into his back pockets. "That's a ridiculous question," he said gruffly, pretending a sudden interest in a flock of seagulls fighting over a few scattered potato chips.

"No, it's not," she argued. "Because if we're really stuck with each another, we ought to at least try to get along. And that's difficult to do when you hate me because I'm rich." She started back up the beach, looking thoughtfully down at the damp sand. "So, I was just trying to get an idea of how much money a person is allowed to have before you begin prejudging her."

Sam knew she was right; what surprised him was her intuitive sense. And the unhappiness he detected in her voice.

"You're exaggerating," he hedged.

She shook her head. "I don't think so." Then she stopped again, tracing circles in the sand with the toe of her sneaker. "May I make a suggestion?"

He shrugged.

Abby wondered what she was doing. Why on earth didn't she leave well enough alone? She'd been insisting she didn't want an intimate relationship with Sam; now she was all but begging for familiarity. Even as she knew she was playing with fire, she realized she couldn't bear the thought of Sam hating her.

"I'll promise to quit thinking of you as an overbearing storm trooper if you try to give me credit for being more than a spoiled rich bitch."

"I never thought of you as that," he protested instantly. "Pampered, perhaps," he allowed, "but no one would ever accuse you of being a bitch." Then, as her words sank in more deeply, his gaze narrowed. "A storm trooper?"

Abby rubbed her palms on the front of her jeans. "Well, you are a little forceful.... Did you say pampered?"

Their gaze held, as each waited for an apology from the other. Then they laughed, and Abby didn't object when Sam put his arm about her shoulder as they made their way up the beach.

"Want to talk about this morning?" he invited after a time.

Abby's rippling sigh told its own story.

"It might do you good to get it off your chest," he suggested.

Abby stared out across the sun-brightened water. "It's just so damn frustrating," she muttered. "I feel as if I'm banging my head against a stone wall every time I try to get funding."

Before Sam could respond, a Frisbee came sailing toward them, landing on the damp sand at their feet. He picked it up, tossing it back to the young man who yelled his thanks. As Sam and Abby watched, he flung it out over the surf, where it was retrieved by an enthusiastic Irish setter.

"Talented dog," Sam observed. "The Dodgers could use him in the outfield."

Abby looked up at him in surprise. "Don't tell me you're a Dodgers fan?" She was inordinately pleased to find something they shared in common.

"Isn't everyone?" he asked with a grin that banished any lingering feelings of resentment she might be harboring.

"Everyone who counts," she agreed with an answering smile.

Lacing his fingers with hers, Sam began walking again. "I liked Marshall's book.... Is it a good screenplay?" he asked suddenly.

"I think so," Abby commented neutrally.

"Who wrote it?"

"I did," she said, waiting for the inevitable remark about actors sticking to what they knew best. That was another reason she'd been given far too often for refusals to even look at her screenplay.

"You really want this, don't you?" he asked instead.

She met his gaze, a warmth flowing through her that had nothing to do with the warm California sun overhead as she viewed the unmasked tenderness in his eyes.

"More than anything," she admitted.

He squeezed her hand. "Then you'll get it."

"How do you know that?"

He brushed a few strands of windblown hair from her face, allowing his fingers to linger on her cheek far longer than was necessary.

"Because I've got faith in you, Abby. Whatever you want out of life, you'll end up getting because you're no quitter."

What if I want you, Sam Garrett, she wondered, feeling for all the world like a besotted teenager suffering her first crush. Then she shook her head. What on earth was the matter with her the past few days? She had enough troubles without inviting the ones inherent in a relationship with the likes of Sam Garrett. She'd definitely been working too hard, Abby decided. What she needed was a long rest. Something that was impossible if she was going to locate funding for *Medicine Woman* before the season's hiatus was over.

Sam had not missed the emotions washing over Abby's face in continuous waves. First desire, then something that resembled fear, followed by that now familiar resolve. The final expression, and the one that lingered on her delicate features was depression, and he sought a way to dispel it.

His roving eye caught sight of a broad red and white umbrella a few yards up the beach. Underneath the shade of the umbrella stood an elderly man whose interested gaze was directed their way.

"Is that the site of the world's best chili dogs?" Sam asked, drawing Abby's attention to the hot dog stand.

"That's it," she said, a smile blooming on her face to banish the earlier clouds. "Get ready for the best lunch you've ever had," she promised, her step quickening along the packed wet sand at the edge of the water.

A smile split the old man's weathered face as she approached. "Abby!"

Abby took off running, hurling herself into his outstretched arms like a rambunctious puppy. She laughed, a relaxed, happy sound Sam hadn't ever heard from her. "Oh, Louie, have I ever missed you!"

"Hey," the vendor protested, "I've been right here, same as always. You're the one who's been too busy to come visit an old man."

Sam watched as Abby pulled off the man's blue Dodgers cap and tousled his white hair. She topped him by at least three inches and they made an odd couple, the wizened old vendor and the beautiful young woman. But something told Sam their relationship went far deeper than a few hot dogs would indicate. Abby hadn't even been this comfortable with her brother, he mused. Of course that could have had something to do with the fact that Kenneth Swan had pulled a gun in her driveway.

"We've been finishing up the season," Abby apologized, replacing the cap atop Louie's head with a fondness Sam fleetingly wished was directed his way.

"Does Jessica get it?" Louie asked, plopping a fat wiener onto a bun, obviously knowing ahead of time what Abby would order.

She wrinkled her nose in what Sam found to be an uncharacteristic, but totally endearing mannerism. "Now, Louie, you know I'm not allowed to reveal the plot of *Potomac* to anyone," she scolded.

"So," he repeated, "does Jessica get it?"

Abby further surprised Sam by revealing yesterday's scene. "Senator Kent's wife shoots her, but nobody knows if she's going to die or not."

"Nobody?" He covered the bun with red chili, sprinkling the chili dog with an ample serving of chopped onions.

"Nobody," she stressed.

"So. You haven't found your money yet."

Abby shook her head and the smile that had been lighting up her face faded. "I need a chili dog fix," she stated, her expression giving him the answer.

"It's been too long since you came for one of Louie's chili dogs." His bright blue eyes surveyed her judiciously. "It looks as if you need extra cheese today. One big gust and you'll blow out to sea." His gaze moved to Sam. "So, who's the boyfriend?"

"He's not a boyfriend," Abby rushed to clarify before Sam could respond.

"Sam Garrett," he stated, shaking the older man's hand. "And I'm working on it."

Louie's weathered face creased into deep furrows as he grinned approval. "That's the boy. This one needs a strong man to look after her."

"That's what I've been telling her," Sam agreed, giving Abby a friendly grin.

"What'll it be?" Louie asked, his gaze moving from Abby to Sam.

"Whatever Abby's having is fine with me."

"She's having Louie Minetti's super special," Louie replied. "With extra everything. Look at her, she's skin and bones. How's she gonna get fattened up enough to have kids, if she don't eat?"

Abby didn't like the way both men were looking at her as if she were an entrant in a dog show and Sam was hoping to win grand prize.

"I was thinking the same thing," Sam stated conversationally. "I got her to eat dinner last night, but you know how stubborn she can be. The woman flatly refused breakfast."

Abby sucked in a harsh, furious breath as she realized how his words must have sounded to Louie. But the older man only winked as he continued to prepare the chili dogs.

"Dinner's a start." Louie handed the cardboard containers to Sam. "You just gotta keep after her. Here, take your lady and put some meat on her bones." He gave Abby an innocent grin. "Have fun, darling."

"You had no right to do that," she fumed as they made their way to a large outcropping of rocks.

"Do what?"

Her eyes were flashing with anger. "You know very well what. You let Louie think we'd spent the night together."

Sam handed her one of the cartons. Then he shrugged, biting into the gooey chili dog. "I didn't say that," he argued when he finished chewing. "But I also didn't see any reason to let the old guy down. He seemed really excited that you showed up with a man in tow." Sam shot her an interested glance. "Is it that unusual?"

It was Abby's turn to feign nonchalance. "I've only ever introduced Louie to two men. You and Ken."

Sam felt inordinately pleased, trying to forget that he had no use for Kenneth Swan and didn't want to be in any group that had Abby's half brother as a member.

"I'm honored," he said truthfully. "How come?"

Abby chewed thoughtfully, savoring the tangy spices that had never failed to lift her spirits. She'd gotten far more from Louie than hot dogs over the years. He'd given her love. Something that all the Swan money had never been able to buy.

"I don't know," she murmured, her gaze directed out to sea. "I think perhaps I didn't want to share him."

Sam understood why Abby had been annoyed when he'd hit it right off with Louie. He'd inadvertantly invaded her turf.

"I didn't mean to spoil your reunion for you."

She shook her head. "You didn't. I was just a little jealous. I've never seen Louie take to anyone like that."

"Not even your half brother?" Sam couldn't make himself say the guy's name aloud.

"Brother," she corrected softly. "No," she admitted on a slight sigh, "that was a little disappointing. I love both of them and I was hoping they'd become friends. But it didn't work out."

"The relationship was doomed to fail, Abby."

"Why?" she asked tartly.

"Because your brother would never stoop to getting sand in his three-hundred-dollar shoes," Sam answered, his face a mask of total seriousness.

Abby's head spun toward him and she stared, trying to read the expression in his eyes. Then her laughter suddenly bubbled over. "You're terrible. Ken adores those shoes."

"That's why he can never visit Louie for chili dogs," Sam explained patiently.

Abby's laughter washed over him like a cool, refreshing stream. "You know what, Sam Garrett?" she asked a little breathlessly.

He reached out, brushing back some windblown strands of hair from her face. "What?"

The smile reached all the way up to her eyes, brightening them to a lustrous silver. "You're good for me," she admitted. "This place is good for me. I'm glad we came here today."

He stroked her cheek with his knuckles. "Me, too," he agreed, fighting the urge to devour those soft, smiling lips. "Me, too."

He could read the answering desire in her eyes and it took a vast amount of effort to force his mind back to business.

"I called the lab while you were in with that banker," he revealed suddenly. "We've traced the stationery your pen pal has been using."

Abby experienced a momentary regret as Sam ignored the opportunity to kiss her. She hadn't meant to invite it, but she was secretly willing to admit that she wouldn't have resisted if he'd tried.

"Really?"

"It's recycled, made in a mill up near Tacoma, Washington."

"You've even found the mill?" Abby asked.

"That was the easy part." He shrugged off her admiring gaze. "It's only made in that one mill, for an environmental group."

His words rang a bell and she turned toward him, her fingers tightening about his forearm. "Sam, I appeared at a fund-raising benefit in Vancouver, Washington, about six months ago."

"I know."

Of course he did, Abby mused. Sam knew everything. "It was shortly after that, that I began getting those letters."

"Right."

He sure didn't sound too enthusiastic, Abby considered. "Well, surely that'll make it easy to find him."

"Washington has a lot of people in it, Abby," he reminded her.

He was only warning her to be cautious, Abby told herself. He didn't want her to get her hopes up. "I know, but how many are environmentalists who live between Vancouver and Tacoma?"

"That's what we're working on now."

Abby tossed some crumbs to the gulls who'd gathered at the foot of her rock. "That's terrific, Sam," she stated excitedly. "You've no idea how much I needed to hear some good news."

He couldn't help feeling guilty as he viewed her enthusiastic face. Let her have this little ray of hope, he decided silently, forcing himself to return her smile. For the time being, he'd have to keep his thoughts to himself.

"Tell me about your half brother."

"My *brother*," she corrected briskly, tossing out another crumb.

"But you had different mothers.

Her eyes turned hard as she looked up at him. "But the same father. The fact that Matthew Swan made two wives miserable does not make me love Ken any less."

His admiring gaze made Abby go a little weak at the knees. "I wonder if he realizes what a lucky man he is?"

"I'm the lucky one," she countered.

"It doesn't bother you that he inherited control of Swan Pharmaceuticals?"

Her gaze was directed at a ship on the horizon. "He didn't," she murmured.

"But he *is* president."

She nodded.

"Look, Abby," Sam protested, growing admittedly frustrated, "I'm not thrilled the way you're dragging this little story out bit by bit."

"And I can't help wondering why you're so interested in Ken," she replied swiftly.

"Because I'm getting the distinct impression that there's some dark family secret concerning the guy. Jordan only hedged on the topic when I brought it up with him."

Abby stifled a small, regretful sigh. "Jordan and Ken don't get along that well," she admitted softly.

"Why doesn't Jordan like him?"

"It's not exactly that. He just didn't approve when I appointed him to the top slot at Swan Pharmaceuticals."

"*You* appointed him?" Sam's tone was incredulous.

"I inherited controlling interest, although I won't receive absolute control until my thirtieth birthday—"

"Which is in three weeks, right?"

"Right," she nodded, not at all surprised Sam knew that little bit of information. "Anyway, I was able to convince the board that Ken was right for the job. He's got an MBA from Harvard; I've never had any interest in the company, other than concern for the employees. If I'd shut down, they'd all have been out of work. But I also had no intention of giving up my work to oversee the manufacturing of prescription drugs."

"Why didn't your father simply will you a generous stock settlement and hand the reins over to your brother, if he was the more qualified?"

"Because Dad had added a codicil to the will denying Ken or his mother a cent from the estate."

Sam's eyebrows rose. "Why?"

"It's a long story. I didn't even know I had a brother, that's how much of a secret he'd kept his first marriage."

"When did you find out?"

"When the will was read," she answered in a flat, dull tone.

Sam reached out, taking her hand. "That must have come as a bit of a shock."

His thumb was tracing little circles on her palm, but his touch was more comforting than seductive, so not only did Abby not pull away, she allowed herself to rest her head on Sam's broad shoulder.

"It was horrible," she admitted. "Jordan probably didn't want to tell you about it because he's always been uncomfortable with the entire idea. He was Dad's attorney before being elected to the senate, and had drawn up both the will and the codicil. But he assured me he'd advised Dad not to be so harsh."

"But your father had his own notions about his first family, and from what I've heard about Matthew Swan, once he made a decision, he was not a man to be easily swayed."

Abby swallowed, the lump in her throat preventing speech. She could still feel the pain and shock of that day nearly a year ago and was surprised that it could still hurt. Sensing her distress, Sam put his free arm around her shoulders.

"So, you hired private detectives, tracked the guy down and handed him your birthright to assuage your misplaced sense of guilt?"

Her eyes flared up at him. "Not exactly. I did hire a private detective to find him. Ken was currently out of work, so I invited him to come to work at Swan. He had a lot of good ideas. It was Ken who made the decision to begin manufacturing generic drugs, something my father would never do."

"How did that work out?"

"Swan had a record quarter. The stockholders are in seventh heaven, and although the board is still griping about me bringing in what they consider an outsider, the company's never been in better financial shape."

"If the guy's such a hotshot businessman, why did Matthew write him out of his will?"

She placed her palm on his thigh as a cloud moved across her thoughtful gaze. Sam tried to ignore the way it felt—as if she was branding him with her gentle touch.

"Ken was simply an innocent victim of a problem between his mother and my father."

"Sounds like more than a problem," Sam remarked with studied casualness.

Abby glanced out to sea. "My father's interests were always directed toward his work," she explained softly. "When he continued to neglect Ken's mother, it was not surprising that she found someone else."

"Some willing man to warm her bed?" His tone was unnecessarily harsh, and although Sam knew his reaction was partially due to his own ill-fated marriage, he didn't retract his statement.

"You're horribly cynical," Abby returned sharply. "There's a lot more to marriage than sex."

"Spoken by the lady who's never taken the plunge," he pointed out.

His gritty words had Abby turning toward him. "Have you ever been married, Sam?"

"Once."

His harsh monosyllable didn't invite her next question, but Abby couldn't resist. "What happened?"

"It didn't work out."

"I suppose that makes you an authority on what makes a good marriage?" she questioned archly.

He responded with a question of his own. "What do you think makes for a happy marriage, Abby?"

"Love," she answered without hesitation.

His laugh was short and more than a little bitter. "Then you're living in Fantasyland, sweetheart. Love is only sex tied up with pretty words. Want me to tell you what marriage really is?"

When she didn't respond, he continued anyway. "Marriage is nothing more than a convenient deal between two people who both have something the other one wants. When the balance of power shifts, it's over. Finished. Kaput."

Instead of becoming angry at his harsh tone, Abby was inexplicably touched by the pain she thought she saw etched on his face. The man's marriage had obviously been a disaster and it seemed to have soured him on the entire idea of love. The fact that Sam could be vulnerable came as an amazing revelation.

Her fingers tightened imperceptibly on his leg, and her eyes softened as she looked up into his tight face. A muscle jerked along his jawline, and it was all that Abby could do not to reach up and smooth away the tension ravaging his features.

He'd have to be blind not to see the shining light in her eyes. Sam could read the lingering curiosity and had the uneasy notion that Abby wasn't going to rest until she'd dragged out the entire sordid story of his marriage. But there was more gleaming in those lustrous pewter depths. There was an unsatisfied passion that would have given him vast satisfaction were it not accompanied by a gentle concern that he took for pity.

He jerked his gaze away from hers and rose suddenly from the rocks. "The tide's coming in," he pointed out gruffly. "If we don't get back, we're going to end up stranded out here."

He was not an easy man to know, Abby thought ruefully. Whenever he let that tough, man-in-charge facade crack just a little, she'd catch a fleeting glimpse of a gentle man, capable of vast amounts of love. But Sam guarded his emotions well and she knew the stone wall he kept erecting between them had taken a lifetime to construct. What on earth made her think she could breach those sturdy parapets in three days? And even more distressing was the question, why did she even want to try?

They remained silent as they wandered back down the beach, the only sound the steady roaring of the oncoming tide, and the strident squalls of the seabirds as they dove for hapless fish in the white-crested waters.

As soon as they entered the house, Sam flung himself onto the sofa, staring moodily out to sea. Opting for a cautious approach, Abby chose a chair across the room. Neither spoke, and the silence grew between them, thicker and thicker, like a heavy morning fog.

"It's not fair," she stated softly, when she couldn't stand the stifling quiet a moment longer.

"What's not fair?"

"That you know almost everything about me, but every time I try to learn one little thing about your life before you showed up at the studio, you turn away."

"It's my job to know everything about you. My past is none of your concern," he said through gritted teeth.

"It's still not fair," she murmured, tracing the bright floral designs on the sailcloth cushion of the chair.

He was off the couch like a shot, crossing the room in two long strides, his fingers tight about her upper arms as he jerked her from the chair.

"You want to know about me, Abby?" he rasped. "Well, I'll tell you everything just this once, then I never want to discuss me again.

"My name is Sam Garrett—just plain Sam, nothing fancy like Samuel—and I'm thirty-nine years old. My father was a dreamer, always chasing that illusive fortune like the gold at the end of the rainbow. Unfortunately, he was also a chronic gambler and an unlucky one at that. When he died, it took us five years to pay off his debts. I went to UCLA on an NROTC scholarship, because it was the only way I could afford to get an education.

"After graduation I paid off that debt with a stint as a marine fighter pilot in Vietnam. I used to have nightmares about those days. I don't anymore. . . . I returned home to find my wife living with some hippie who'd burned his draft card. Needless to say, neither one of them was thrilled to see I'd managed to return in one piece.

"But that was okay by me, because I wasn't exactly delighted to see them, either. The only thing that really burned me up was that I'd been sending money home to buy that creep drugs and cheap wine. I didn't bother to unpack; I left the house and never saw either one of them again.

"I've worked for the Bureau for the past fourteen years, and although I've shot at men, and been shot myself, I've never killed anyone on the job. That's not to say there haven't been a lot who didn't deserve it.

"I'm not a man who gives pretty speeches, but I want you, Abby Swan, more than any woman I've ever known."

The harsh, angry declaration had taken her breath away, and as she stared up at him, Abby knew without any doubt that Sam was about to kiss her. She braced herself for a blazing onslaught of passion as his head swooped down, but was stunned by the gentleness of his lips as they covered hers. Although his lips barely brushed hers, the effect was cataclysmic as a surge of desire rocked her to the very center of her being. Brilliant colors exploded behind her closed eyelids, and she heard a ragged moan, unaware it was her own. Then his mouth came down on hers, crushingly, hungrily, and she heard nothing.

Passion had tastes; as her lips moved under his, Abby drank in the rich, dark flavor of his mouth, finding it to be more stimulating, more intoxicating than hot, mulled wine. It had scents; she breathed in the warm leather of his aftershave, the tangy scent of salt air in his hair, and a heady male aroma that sent her head spinning.

An illusive passion she'd never before experienced whipped through her, warming her blood, melting her bones, bringing her to the edge of reason, then carrying her beyond, as the heat grew almost too intense to bear.

Sam's long fingers cupped the back of her head, denying her freedom from the desperation of his mouth. His lips plucked at hers, his tongue traced a trail of fire, his teeth took nips at her bottom lip. It was as if he'd been starving his entire life, and Abby's soft lips were the sweetest of fruits. He dragged his mouth from hers, pressing hard, stinging kisses along her jawline, up the slanted line of her cheekbone to her temple, where he could almost taste the wild beat of her blood.

As his lips moved over her face, Abby's lashes fluttered, coming to rest on her cheeks, and he kissed her closed lids. Then his lips returned to hers, the kiss far more passionate than gentle as Abby kissed him back, heatedly, furiously.

Her hunger fed Sam's own, making him desperate to touch all of her, to taste her, to explore every glorious inch of her burning, yielding body. Impatient with the clothing that separated them, he tore at the buttons of her blouse, pulling the material aside, dispatching the front clasp of her lacy bra with a single deft stroke.

His touch on her flesh electrified her and Abby cried out, even as her own hands tugged at Sam's shirt, pulling it free of his jeans. Her palms pressed against his chest, her fingers tangled in the rich dark mat of chestnut hair, her roving touch drawing a deep groan that Abby could feel against her fingertips.

Sam pressed kisses across her shoulder blades, down the soft slope of her breasts. His palms caressed that satiny flesh, causing them to swell to fit his hands, making his mind take off on a fleeting, highly erotic fantasy. Would everything between them be such a close and perfect fit, he wondered, stroking her burgeoning nipples with a steady, circular motion until they were hard and erect.

Abby buried her face in his shoulder, soft moans escaping her lips as Sam continued his erotic caresses on her incredibly sensitive nipples.

"Do you like that?" he murmured, his tongue stroking her ear as his hands continued to torment her aching breasts.

"You know I do," she whispered, taking a deep breath as one hand continued downward, splayed against her rib cage. "I don't understand what you do to me," she protested, her legs weakening as that roving, treacherous hand moved ever steadily downward.

"Don't try to understand. Just enjoy." His crisp dark hair brushed her skin as he bent his head, capturing one taut bud between his lips and tugging.

"Oh, Sam," she sighed, her passion-laced voice tinged with a faint hint of regret.

Feeling her vacillation, Sam sought to dispel it. "No, don't fight it, Abby. I want you, sweetheart. It's been so long. Too long."

He was referring to how long he'd wanted her, how many sleepless nights he'd spent imagining Abby lying in his arms, her soft, fluid body pressed against his. He realized Abby had taken it all wrong as she stiffened momentarily, fighting the desire raging through her like a red-hot wind.

Of course, she told herself. Sam had told her about those long months in the hospital. It would stand to reason such a virile man would be in need of a woman. Any woman.

"Next time, perhaps you'd better get your relief from one of those friendly nurses more versed in bedside manner before you check out of the hospital," she said, trying to pull away.

Sam's arms tightened around her, refusing to allow her escape. An errant voice in the back of his mind told him to tell Abby the truth—that while he'd admittedly been without a woman for a very long time, his physical needs were nothing when compared to what he felt for her. But old habits die hard and Sam found himself unable to admit his complex need for her, and her alone.

"What makes you think I was celibate the entire time I was in the hospital?" he challenged, his words reckless, his tone taunting.

His fingers cupped the soft curves of her buttocks, bringing her closer to the hard evidence of his arousal. Abby bit her lip at the flood of passion the close contact evoked.

Of course Sam would never have difficulty finding a woman to make love to, she considered. Correction, have sex with. Hadn't he professed only a short time before that love was only sex wrapped up with pretty words? She hated to think herself capable of a purely physical response. There had to be more involved in her feelings for Sam. Didn't there?

"This is too soon," she protested, even as she leaned into him, fitting her soft curves to his hard length.

His hands pressed against the small of her back. "No it's not. Trust me, Abby."

She did, she realized. She trusted Sam with her life. There was a bond slowly being forged between them. A bond far stronger, far more lasting than a night of casual sex would indicate.

She tried to make him understand. "It'll just complicate things."

His lips covered hers, as if to smother a denial. "No it won't. It'll make things easier. If I'm supposed to be watching out for you, think how simpler that will be if we're sharing a bed."

His desperation made his words rash and Sam regretted them the moment he heard them escape. He'd never mixed sex and work before. His professional relationships and his private ones had been kept separate, for obvious reasons. Only Abby had made him shatter that long-held tenet.

As much as every nerve ending in her body was on red alert, crying out for release, Abby couldn't help wondering if this was standard operating procedure for Sam Garrett. Had he spent his free time lying with some bronze-skinned beauty on that Caribbean island, forging his own good-neighbor policy? Had he experienced the pleasure found in whatever women existed in that shadowy, mysterious realm of the underworld? Did sex and danger go hand in hand for Sam, each in its own way undeniably exciting?

"What are they called?" she asked softly.

He was nibbling at her neck. "Who?"

She closed her eyes to the delicious things his hands were doing to her body. "Gangsters' girlfriends," she explained in a ragged tone. "Do they still call them molls?"

What was she getting at? "Nope." His teeth nipped at her earlobe.

Abby pushed tentatively against his shoulders, discovering that she might as well try to budge the Rock of Gibraltar. "Then what are they called?"

"Inmates," he responded shortly, wanting to end this conversation. He could feel the golden cloud of desire that had surrounded them slowly dissipating. "At least the ones I arrested are. Women's lib might be a little slower in that part of society, but some of them have managed to make inroads.... Why?" he asked, genuinely curious as to the reason for her continued questioning.

"I was just thinking of you making love with them and realized that if gangsters are now racketeers, I didn't know what to call their girlfriends."

So that's the way the wind blows, Sam thought wearily. For some reason it was important that Abby understand this had been an aberration. That she was special.

He tilted his head back, his eyes suddenly sober. "I never went to bed with any of them, Abby. In fact, I've never gotten involved with any women I met through my work."

She might be ready to trust this man with her life, but she wasn't prepared to buy that line. "Sure."

"You don't believe me." His tone was flat.

"Why should I?"

Why indeed, he agreed silently. His words were insisting one thing, even as his actions led her to suspect the worst. He sighed, moving a little away as he refastened her ivory bra and began to slowly, regretfully, button her blouse.

"Because I've never felt about a woman like I feel about you," he answered honestly.

At her bemused look, he shook his head. "It's not exactly what I would have chosen, either," he admitted. "It's impossible for me to be with you and not want you, Abby. But I won't push the issue."

Then he gave her a crooked smile. "The trick is to find other things to occupy our time."

She folded her arms across her aching breasts in an unconsciously protective gesture. "So what do you suggest? Playing dominoes or checkers until your partner takes over your shift?"

"How about letting me read your screenplay?"

Abby couldn't help staring at him, wondering if she had only imagined that casually issued suggestion. "My screenplay? You mean the one for *Medicine Woman*?"

The smile extended to his eyes. "Do you have any others?"

She shook her head. "No, that's the only one." Her gray eyes narrowed. "Do you really want to read it?"

"I'd love to read it. If you don't mind," he tacked on almost hesitantly.

His seeming lack of self-assurance made him appear almost vulnerable once again, and Abby had to restrain herself from flinging her arms around his neck.

"I'd love you to read my screenplay, Sam," she said, her answering smile lighting up the room. "I'll go get it for you."

Sam watched her leave the room, both her step and her mood lighter than he'd seen since he began tailing her nearly three weeks ago. Inexplicably, Abby's good humor seemed to lighten his own spirits and as he thrust his hands into his pockets and stared out at the sailboats bobbing on the sapphire waters, he felt his own mouth curving into a wide, idiotic grin.

7

ABBY PACED THE FLOOR of her living room impatiently waiting for Sam to finish reading the screenplay of *Medicine Woman*. Although she didn't know exactly why she should feel so strongly about it, it suddenly became very important that he like her film. That he thought it possessed true merit. He'd been out on her terrace for the last hour, and if he didn't say something soon, she was going to scream.

Finally, deciding she had to direct all this energy into something more constructive, she sat down at a white wicker desk in the corner of the room, determined to concentrate on the film's budget instead of the frustratingly silent man outside.

As Sam read the screenplay, he found it easy to imagine Abby in the role of the young idealistic doctor who packed up her black bag to practice medicine in the hill country of West Virginia.

At first the heroine responded as expected to the old woman who'd practiced herbal healing for nearly fifty years among the hill folk. There were the inevitable fireworks when science met mountain folklore. But gradually, the young woman learned to appreciate the other's knowledge, and by the end of the film the two women had formed a close bond, working together as they shared their talents.

Abby was a great deal like that, he mused. She possessed an iron will that was tempered by the silken threads of her sensitivity. She was undeniably idealistic—look at what she'd done for her half brother—yet she was pragmatic enough not to burn her bridges behind her by giving up *Potomac* while seeking the funds to produce this project. She was vastly independent, and while he'd found that an irritating quality more than once in the past few days, it was a personality trait Sam knew the two of them shared.

It was coming as a discomforting surprise to him that not only did he want Abby very much, he also admired her. While she admittedly brought out a strong protective streak in him, he liked the way she insisted on standing on her own two feet. For the first time in a very long while, Sam had imagined sharing his life with a woman. Which was ironic, because he couldn't have found a less likely individual if he'd tried.

"It's going to be a dynamite film," he said, returning to the living room.

Abby looked up from the pile of ledger sheets she'd been poring over.

"You sure sound a lot more positive about it ever being made than I do," she said with a slightly weary sigh.

He reached down to massage the muscles at the back of her neck. She was tense. So very tense. "I've got faith in you."

His words, as well as his gently kneading touch, made Abby feel worlds better. She wondered idly when she'd gone from not wanting Sam Garrett in her life to enjoying his company very much. He had incredible patience, she mused, envying him that character trait.

Too many times over the past three days she'd looked up to find him watching her, waiting. While he still reminded her of a hawk circling its prey, Abby knew Sam wouldn't force her into anything she wasn't ready for. That knowledge had enabled her to relax and enjoy his company now.

"They make me so damn mad," she muttered. "Can you believe that stuffy banker was holding out for a share of Swan Pharmaceuticals?"

"Now that I've read the screenplay, I can't see why you're rejecting that offer," he admitted. "It'll be a great movie, Abby. You're bound to make money."

She looked up at him, her grave eyes trying to make him understand. "I don't want to use my father's money to ensure my own success, Sam. I want—no, I need—to do it myself."

"You will be doing it yourself," he argued.

"You're just as bad as the rest of them," she grumbled, turning back to her accounting sheets. He felt the loosened muscles tensing once again under his fingertips. "Do you mind?" she inquired sharply. "I'm trying to concentrate."

Knowing that Abby's frustration was directed at her problem, and not him, Sam dropped his hands obediently and crossed the room, sitting on the blue and white sailcloth-covered couch. Beyond the glass wall, the sun was setting, turning the waters to flaming gold and he remained silent as he watched the surf breaking on shore and waited.

He didn't have to wait long. Giving in to the long silence, Abby sighed lightly and crossed the room to the couch. She joined him in watching the waves for a time, marshaling her thoughts.

"You have to understand," she said finally, as she stared out to sea, "that to my father, money was power. He wielded it over everyone."

"Including you."

She nodded.

"How about your brother? He doesn't seem averse to living on Swan money."

Abby laughed at that one, but it was not the bubbly light sound he'd come to love. It was a dry, harsh sound he hated to hear coming from her lips. "Oh, Father used his money against Ken, too; he just never thought I'd have the guts to do anything about it."

"I'm surprised, if your father was that ruthless, that Ken's mother made the mistake of getting caught. Surely she'd know Matthew wouldn't be thrilled with the idea of another man in bed with his wife."

Abby shrugged. "He didn't love her, why should he have taken it so badly?"

"You've a lot to learn about men, Abby," Sam taunted her lightly. "There's a little matter of pride involved. If a man is willing to go to all the trouble to marry a woman, to give her his name, he expects her to at least remain his private property."

"Property?" Abby exploded. "What a chauvinistic, twelfth-century notion! You make women sound like nothing but chattel."

Sam's intent eyes watched her breasts rise and fall under the soft gauze. He knew Abby would probably toss him out on his ear if he mentioned it, but she was damn gorgeous when she was angry.

She glared at him, enraged even further by the unmistakable gleam of desire sparking in the depths of his eyes. "Well, let me tell you, Sam Garrett," she professed, jabbing her finger in the air, "I'm just glad I found this out about you before . . . before . . . Oh, skip it," she muttered.

"Before we went to bed together?" Sam finished for her. "Don't worry, Abby, I certainly don't want you trailing ten feet behind me." He grinned at her wickedly. "I much prefer my women to take an equal part in lovemaking; you'll encounter no chauvinism in the bedroom, sweetheart."

"You're disgusting!"

"I told you not to expect pretty speeches from me."

"I'll keep that in mind," she retorted, turning her head away.

"You still haven't explained why you don't use the stock as collateral," he reminded her.

She pulled her knees to her chest, wrapping her arms around them. "*Medicine Woman* is going to be my success," she stated firmly. "Not Matthew Swan's."

An idea had been germinating in Sam's mind for the past hour, but he didn't feel free to reveal it to Abby just yet.

"How about dinner?" he asked suddenly.

Abby shook her head. "I'm not hungry."

"All you've had all day is that chili dog," he pointed out. "I promised Louie I'd see that you ate."

"It seems to me that you're pretty quick to hand out promises about my life," she responded tartly.

He shrugged, pushing up from the couch. "I'll fix us something to eat."

"You don't have to do that," she argued.

Sam jammed his hands into his back pockets, his irritation rising to new heights. "Look, Abby, I'm starving. Now I'm going to make myself something to eat. Do you want me to make enough for two or not?"

Abby remained silent as she considered his question. There was something almost too intimate about the idea of Sam cooking dinner for her. He seemed determined to take over all aspects of her life, and while she was the first to admit she'd appreciated his strength this morning, both before and after her meeting with James Palmer, she couldn't allow his intervention to become a habit. What would she do when he was gone?

"Well?" he prompted, no trace of sympathy softening his tone.

"All right," she snapped.

"Good," he agreed, outwardly ignoring her spark of anger as he sauntered into the kitchen.

Stifling an oath, Abby returned to her ledger sheets, determined to put Sam Garrett from her mind.

Sam forced himself to go slow on the Scotch as he prepared a light supper. Damn her, anyway, he considered blackly, banging the pans around with unnecessary force. Abby's insistence on total autonomy was going to drive him crazy.

That wasn't it, he admitted, pouring another splash of Scotch into the old-fashioned crystal glass. He was storming around here because she was effectively managing to keep him at arm's length, despite his efforts to the contrary. She was nearly thirty years old, nine years younger than he was, yet there had been too many times when he'd felt like an awkward adolescent boy trying to get the nerve to ask a girl to the prom.

"Hi."

The soft greeting shattered his dark thoughts and Sam turned to view Abby standing in the doorway.

"How about a drink?" he asked.

She eyed the glass of Scotch in his hand. No way, Abby decided. Drinking anything that strong with this man around would be asking for trouble.

"I think I'll settle for a glass of wine," she said, moving past him toward the refrigerator. "There was a bottle in here before the fire, perhaps it's still there."

"It is," he agreed. "Why don't you just sit down and put your feet up and I'll get it for you."

"I can get my own wine."

"Of course you can," he pointed out, "but you've been working hard most of the day. Sit down and relax." He pulled out a chair at the table.

Deciding to save her arguing for more important issues, Abby complied, watching as he retrieved the bottle and poured the wine into a tall stemmed glass. He'd rolled his sleeves up and her gaze was directed to his well-muscled forearms. He was an undeniably strong man, but she had the feeling he knew how to be gentle, when the situation called for it. Knowing such thoughts were dangerous, she couldn't help wondering what it would be like to be made love to by such a man.

"How many people have you approached for funding?" he asked casually, putting a pat of butter into the small skillet.

"Scads," she muttered, as she watched him stir the omelet. The man definitely knew his way around a kitchen.

He swirled the pan around with one hand while dumping some ingredients from a cutting board into the skillet with the other. "How about Torr Janzen?"

Her eyes narrowed as she shot him a long, appraising glance. "How do you know about him?"

"I grew up in this town, Abby. While I admittedly don't read the trade papers, it'd be a little hard not to have heard of Torr Janzen."

That was true, she reflected. Torr Janzen was said to have the Midas touch when it came to the movie industry. His secret was that he never went into production until he'd first established video cassette rights, marketing rights, and whatever spinoff sales the project might encourage. His last major undertaking had been *Star Seekers*, a space-adventure story, and he'd earned back every cent of his money from the toy sales alone before the film even appeared in the theaters. Of course she'd tried to interest him in *Medicine Woman*.

"He wouldn't even grant me an appointment," she admitted.

He tipped the omelet onto a plate. "I've heard the guy's a bit of a chauvinist, but you could have sent him the screenplay," Sam suggested offhandedly as he brought the plate to the table. He cut the omelet in half, placing her share on a small plate in front of her. "Eat your dinner before it gets cold," he instructed casually, ignoring the anger that flashed across her face.

"I'm not stupid, Sam. Of course I sent it to him."

"And?"

"And nothing. I received a polite little form letter telling me that he didn't think the project was marketable the way it was." She grimaced. "Now if I moved the heroine to outer space, dressed her in a gold lamé jumpsuit and had her fighting off aliens and going to bed with half the fleet, he probably would've jumped at the chance."

Hearing the frustration in her voice, Sam decided to drop the subject for now. He gave her a mock stern look. "Hey, if you're going to get uptight about the project, let's just forget it while you eat your share of Garrett's world-famous Denver omelet."

Sam appeared determined to ignore Abby's ill temper as he dove into his dinner, appearing quite satisfied with his culinary efforts. Stifling a sigh, she took a bite, inexplicably irritated further when she discovered it to be delicious.

"You're a good cook," she allowed finally.

"Any lady who can get excited about chili dogs is a lousy food critic."

"I'm sorry I snapped at you," she said softly.

Sam shrugged it off. "I can understand how you'd be frustrated, Abby. But I've got faith in you. You'll pull this thing off and after *Medicine Woman* is a smashing success, everyone in this town will be knocking down your door, trying to get you to produce their newest hit."

His sincere tone made her smile. "You can be a nice man, Sam Garrett. When you're not acting like a storm trooper."

He grinned, that devastatingly boyish grin that transformed the craggy features of his face and did funny things to her heart. "You're not so bad yourself, Abby Swan. When you're not spitting like a wet cat."

Although she found the comparison more than a little distasteful, Abby secretly admitted she'd been more touchy than usual lately. But she'd always felt the need to be in control of all aspects of her life. These days she was finding that more and more of an impossibility.

"Why don't you go in the other room and try to relax," he suggested with an encouraging smile. "It'll only take a few minutes to do the dishes."

"You don't have to do them," she protested.

He reached across the table, covering her hand with his. "I know. But I like doing things for you, Abby. And since I don't happen to have twenty million dollars burning a hole in my wallet, at least let me try to make things a little easier for you."

She found the soft light in his tawny eyes impossible to resist. A nice man, she repeated to herself, unable to believe he was honestly as hard-boiled as he seemed to want her to think.

"Thank you," she said. "I've got another meeting tomorrow morning and I'd like to prepare for it."

He patted her hand. "You'll get your money, Abby."

Abby thought she'd detected a promise in those smoothly grave tones. Then, deciding that was ridiculous, she shook her head, rising from the table. "It may just be that you're crazier than I am, Sam."

"Could be," he replied easily, not willing to admit that same thought had crossed his mind more than once over the past three days. Because he had to be out of his mind to be even considering the thoughts he was having about Abby.

There's no future here, Garrett, he told himself, plunging his hands into the soapy water once she'd left the room. *So smarten up and return to the real world.* But as he washed the few utensils, it crossed Sam's mind that he'd spent his entire life being responsible for others. His family, his country, the agency. Just once, he'd like to allow himself the luxury of doing something totally impractical. And getting involved with Abby Swan definitely fit into that category.

Muttering under his breath, Sam reminded himself that Abby had enough problems without him screwing up her life even more. She was an anachronism in this town of hedonistic pleasures. His investigation had determined that she never attended the glittering but decadent Hollywood parties where sex, drugs and booze constituted an evening's entertainment. She appeared to live the life of a hermit—or a nun—he considered, knowing her to eschew the casual sex found in one-night stands. And that was all he could offer her, Sam knew. As much as he longed to lay the world at her feet, all he could give Abby would be a few hours of fleeting pleasure. She deserved more than that.

Even knowing all that, Sam was discovering that he couldn't stay away from her. He couldn't leave her alone. While their time together was admittedly limited, he didn't want to give up a single minute that he could spend with Abby. Damning himself for being a selfish bastard, Sam dried his hands on a paper towel and picked up the telephone.

"Johnny," he said as the phone was picked up on the tenth ring, "I'm glad I caught you."

"I was just out the door," the older man explained. "What's up?"

"Good news," Sam responded with feigned casualness. "You won't have to spend any more lonely nights in your car."

"Then you've closed the case?"

"No," Sam admitted reluctantly. "Nothing's changed."

There was a long thoughtful pause on the other end of the line. "I see," Johnny said finally.

"It's not like that," Sam protested, knowing what was going through his old friend's mind.

"Sam," Johnny said with a fond, paternalistic tone, "we've known each other a long time. Long enough not to have to play games with each other.... She's a lovely woman, and although I would have enjoyed having you for a son-in-law, I think Abby can make you happy." Sam heard the smile in the man's voice. "Go for it, Garrett. And good luck."

He hung up before Sam could respond and as he replaced the receiver on the wall phone, Sam realized that whatever happened this evening, there would be no turning back.

Abby's head was bent over several sheets of paper, her hair an ebony silk curtain hiding her face. Sam wondered how she'd react when she discovered what he'd just done. He sat down on the couch, trying to find a way to tell her. The minutes ticked by, the muffled roar of the surf outside the window the only sound in the room. Abby continued to work, seemingly oblivious to Sam's growing tension.

"Would you like a drink?" he asked abruptly.

She shook her head, making a notation in the margin of one of the ledger sheets. "I don't think so."

"Can I get you anything? Some more wine? Coffee?"

She looked up, rubbing the back of her neck in a weary gesture. "I'd love a cup of tea," she said. "I always have a cup before I go to bed. I know what they say about it being crammed full of caffeine, but it always seems to calm me down."

"And you need calming down now?"

One glance at his eyes was enough to shake her to her toes. They were gleaming with a devastating fire, the heat reaching across the room to engulf her. *All I have to do is look at the man and I'm a goner*, she thought in amazement.

"I think so," she whispered as an unmistakable message passed between them.

Sam knew that if he was to pull this thing off, he couldn't allow himself to get sidetracked with the shared yearning he was viewing on Abby's softened features.

"I'll get the tea," he said in response.

Abby offered him a weak smile. "Thank you."

He didn't answer as he left the room and she leaned her head back and closed her eyes, taking several deep, calming breaths.

Sam found the tea bags without any trouble, welcoming an opportunity to plan their conversation to his liking. He knew without a single doubt that Abby wasn't going to react well to his latest decision. The trick was not to give her any choice, without making it look as if he was taking total control away from her. And that, he considered grimly, could well be the most difficult assignment he'd ever taken on.

The kettle began to whistle, demanding his attention. He fixed her tea, poured himself another Scotch and took both down the hallway to the living room. As he paused near Abby's desk, something occurred to him.

"Did you say you always have a cup of tea before you go to bed?"

"That's right," she answered. "Why?"

"How many people know that?"

She shrugged. "As many who read the profile on me in *People* magazine a few months ago. They sent out a reporter who followed me around for three days. I thought I'd go crazy before he finally left."

"Well," he said, handing her the cup and saucer, "it was a good idea while it lasted."

"Do you think you could explain that?"

He took a sip of his Scotch. "I was just thinking about that burner being turned on after you went to bed. I was hoping only a handful of people knew about the tea. It would give more credence to the fact that it was someone you knew."

"You still don't believe that it's just a looney fan, do you?" Abby asked.

"Let's just say the entire thing has been a little too pat from the beginning. Including the fact that the paper is only available from that one mill. Hell, Abby, if you were going to send someone death threats, wouldn't you use something a little less traceable?"

"Not if I were crazy to begin with," she countered.

"Perhaps," he acknowledged, still unconvinced. There had been something nagging at the back of his mind from the beginning. Something that just didn't fit.

"Do you honestly believe a friend could be writing those letters? And causing these accidents?" Abby asked incredulously.

Sam's expression was set in stone. "Or someone who used to be a friend."

Abby didn't miss the question in his gritty tone. "Are you asking me how many lovers I've had, Sam?" she inquired calmly.

"No." As he muttered the monosyllable, Sam realized that had indeed been what he was doing.

"Good," she murmured, sipping her tea.

When Abby didn't elaborate, Sam experienced a sudden urge to shake her until her lovely teeth rattled. "You look tired," he said instead.

Abby nodded. "I am."

"Perhaps you should go up to bed."

"I will," she agreed readily. "As soon as you leave."

Well, Sam considered, it was now or never. "I'm not leaving," he stated with outward calm.

Abby's eyes flew to his face. "What did you say?"

"I said I'm not leaving."

"Well, you're certainly not staying here," she said briskly.

"Johnny can't come tonight."

"Oh? And when did you discover that little nugget of information?"

"I just spoke with him."

"I didn't hear the phone ring," she challenged.

"I called him. To tell him he could take over any time," Sam ad-libbed the lie, knowing Abby would hit the roof if she knew he'd orchestrated Johnny O'Neill's absence.

"And why can't he come?" she questioned, not quite believing Sam's story. It was too convenient. "And don't tell me he's sitting up with a sick friend."

"Close. His daughter had a baby the other day and she came home from the hospital tonight."

"To his home? Doesn't she have a husband to take care of her?"

"He's in the navy. As we speak, Ernie is somewhere out in the Pacific on maneuvers."

Abby's eyes narrowed. "What did she name the baby?" she asked suddenly, not believing there was a daughter in the first place, let alone a new baby.

"Samantha."

Abby shook her head. "Come on, you can't expect me to buy this, Sam. *Samantha*?"

"Mary and I grew up together. I was the big brother she never had."

"Oh." That much, at least had the ring of truth, Abby determined. "This is ridiculous," she objected.

"I promised Jordan I'd stay with you until we catch the guy writing you those letters," he said quietly.

"What about your own work?"

He shrugged. "I told you, I'm on a temporary leave of absence. I've got a lot of sick leave compiled and I told the agency that I'd be back once we got this little problem all wrapped up."

"Are you always this bossy?"

"Always. Are you always this argumentative?"

"Never. I'm usually a very agreeable person. I think you bring out my bad side, Sam Garrett."

Her eyes were flashing with angry silver lights and Sam couldn't help smiling at how appealing Abby was when she allowed glimpses of her tautly controlled passion.

"Want to take a swing at me?"

Abby shook her head, fighting down the impulse to do exactly that. "You'll have to spend the night in your car," she insisted firmly.

"Abby, do you know what the night air does to my leg?" It was dirty pool, using her own softheartedness against her, but Sam was rewarded as her eyes filled with concern.

"All right," she said with a sigh. "You can stay here. Just for tonight. In the guest room," she tacked on firmly.

"Thank you," he answered gravely. "I do appreciate your hospitality, Abby."

"I'm probably making the biggest mistake of my life," she muttered, "but right now I'm too tired to worry about it. Just remember, it's only for one night. Tomorrow there's no reason why Johnny's daughter can't be left alone. Maneuvers or no maneuvers."

He nodded, wondering what Abby would say when she discovered he had no intention of leaving until the case was closed. "Fair enough. Now why don't you get some sleep before you drop?"

While the last thing Sam wanted right now was to go up to that lonely bed, he wasn't about to press his case and end up out on the street. He knew she'd only agreed to his presence in the first place because Jordan Winston's opinion carried so much weight. And this move tonight was undeniably risky. After a good night's sleep, there was a fair chance of finding her less agreeable to this arrangement.

There was no point in stacking the deck against his plans by insisting on an intimacy she was not prepared to allow, he warned himself. Although every bit of past experience assured him Abby shared his desire, she was not a woman willing to settle for a few hours of casual pleasure. And he had nothing else to offer. For now, they were at a stalemate. Looping his arm about her shoulder in a friendly, harmless manner, Sam reminded himself that patience was a virtue.

"Come on," he said, shepherding her from the room. "It's time we called it a night."

Abby allowed his arm to remain around her as they climbed the stairs, stopping in front of her bedroom. "I still don't see why I need twenty-four-hour protection," she grumbled.

"I want to be close to you, Abby. In case you need me."

Oh, she needed him all right. That was precisely the problem. "I'm not sure this is such a good idea," she murmured.

"If you're so concerned about your virtue being sullied, you can always lock your door," he suggested.

"I could simply say no," she reminded him.

Sam suddenly fixed her with a warm gaze that spoke volumes. "Do you think that would really work?"

"Wouldn't it?" she tossed back.

His head was closer than she'd thought. His eyes dark and dangerous as they settled on her mouth. "It would depend on whether or not you meant it," he said huskily.

Abby blinked, masking the thick flow of desire warming her blood as that slow unsettling smile curved his lips. "Oh, I'd mean it, all right."

Without removing his eyes from hers, he lifted her hand to his lips, pressing a warm kiss in the center of her palm. Abby tried to ignore the sudden increase in her pulse rate.

"Think so?" he challenged, watching the suppressed desire build in her eyes.

It would be so easy. Her slightly parted lips reminded him of lush ripe cherries, ready to be plucked. With just a little effort, he could be making love to Abby, experiencing the pleasure of her soft feminine body under his.

But then what? Where did they go from there? Did he compromise Jordan Winston's trust and Abby's safety by whiling away the hours in her bed, while outside these walls she was being relentlessly stalked by someone who had gotten reality confused with fantasy? That idea brought up another just as unattractive. Is that what he'd done? Had he confused her screen image with the soft vulnerable woman whose intense, silvery eyes were locked to his?

Sam released her hand. "Sleep," he said firmly. "We both need some sleep."

"Sleep," she echoed, not sounding any more pleased with the idea than he was.

His head swooped down, giving her a far too circumspect kiss. "Good night, Abby," he stated with a weary sigh.

She opened her bedroom door. "'Night, Sam," she murmured.

Sam stood in the hallway until the door closed in his face. Then, muttering a low oath, he walked the few feet to his own bedroom, hearing the click as Abby locked her door. He lay awake for a long time, wondering what masochistic impulse had made him come up with this stupid idea in the first place.

8

WHEN ABBY AWOKE the next morning, her first thoughts were of Sam. What on earth was she going to do? She stared up at the ceiling, as if hoping to find some answers in the white stucco swirls. The obvious answer was to move him out of her house. Now. For despite her vow not to become involved, she was drawn to him with an uncommon force and knew that, were they to remain under the same roof, an affair was inevitable.

Would that be so bad, she wondered. What would be so wrong in allowing herself the pleasure Sam could bring into her life? Nothing, she decided, if that was all that would happen. But every feminine instinct Abby possessed told her that Sam was not a man to offer a woman any type of commitment. He'd obviously been burned the first time and had no intention of sampling the matrimonial waters again.

Not that she wanted to marry him, she assured herself. She just didn't want to settle for a few fleeting nights of pleasure, knowing how she'd miss him when he was gone.

She hit the mattress with her fist. "Enough," she demanded. "All you have to do is go downstairs and insist that he leave your house. How difficult could that be?"

She must have been more exhausted than she'd realized to let the man force his way into her life in the first place. She'd just calmly tell him that she appreciated his concern, but he'd have to go.

And if he wouldn't, she mused, as she took her shower. What if he just sat down and refused to move?

"Ridiculous," she muttered, blowing her hair dry. It was still her house. He couldn't possibly stay if she didn't allow him to. And if worse came to worst, she could always call the police.

As she dressed, Abby wondered how enthusiastic the Malibu police would be about evicting an FBI agent. It would probably make the papers. Terrific, suddenly her personal life was getting as outrageous as Jessica Thorne's.

She shook her head, refusing to acknowledge the possibility that Sam wouldn't simply go upstairs and pack once she explained things reasonably. Reminding herself about the power of positive thinking, Abby went downstairs, following the rich scent of brewing coffee.

When she entered the kitchen, she was not surprised to find him already up, dressed once again in the three-piece gray suit of a professional FBI agent. Although he hadn't yet donned the jacket, Abby decided she much preferred him in the faded shirt and jeans of yesterday. He appeared far less formidable.

"I like that outfit," he commented with a welcoming smile. "It makes you look like a brilliant flame."

She brushed an imaginary spot of lint off the scarlet linen. "Red always gives me confidence," she said. "You don't think it makes me look too aggressive?"

Sam knew that under normal conditions Abby would not be seeking advice on her clothing. She had far too much self-confidence to need anyone's approval. But these were far from ordinary circumstances.

"Assertive," he corrected.

"I didn't do too well with feminine yesterday," she admitted with a wry half smile. "I thought I'd try something at the other end of the scale."

He decided this was not the time to point out Abby could look alluring and feminine in a burlap bag. "Sleep well?" he asked casually.

"Like a rock. How about you?"

"Great," he lied, handing her a cup of coffee. "I've already eaten, but I can make you something."

"Thanks, coffee's fine."

"You sure?"

Abby was trying to think of a way to politely ask Sam to leave and his friendly attitude was only making things more difficult. "I told you yesterday that I don't eat breakfast," she snapped. "Okay?"

He looked surprised, but didn't comment on her flash of ill temper. Instead, he only shrugged. "Sure."

They continued to drink their coffee without speaking and Abby was almost relieved when the shrill command of the telephone fractured the thick silence.

"That'll probably be Jordan," Sam advised her as she jumped from her chair to answer it. "I put a call in to him this morning."

"Hello?" she asked briskly, taking out her discomfort with the situation on the caller.

"Abby?"

"Oh, Jordan," she said with a sigh, "you've no idea how happy I am you called."

"So, what do you think?"

"About what?"

He chuckled. "About the Prince Charming I sent you, of course."

He'd remembered. Abby smiled. "I'd say you're a little off the mark with this one."

"Give the guy time, Abby. I think he'll grow on you."

Oh, Jordan, Abby considered weakly, *if you only knew.* "About that, what in the world made you think I needed a baby-sitter?"

"I think you need a lot more than that," Jordan advised dryly. "And as far as I'm concerned, Sam Garrett just about covers the list."

"I don't need a matchmaker, either," she stated firmly, earning an interested glance from Sam.

Jordan expelled a deep sigh of frustration and Abby could envision him combing his hands through his silvery hair. "Look, I'm worried about you. Sam's more than an old friend; he's a senior agent, expert in his field and he agrees those accidents are damn suspicious."

"Even so," she argued, "this is an impossible arrangement. I can't have a man staying here with me, Jordan."

"Why not? It's a big enough house. And in your neighborhood, Abby, no tongues will wag if you have a man living there."

"That's beside the point. I have work to do."

"He won't interfere with that," Jordan pointed out reasonably. "Sam's just there for your protection."

Abby muttered a low oath. "This is ridiculous."

"Is he there with you now?"

She glared over at Sam. He didn't have to look so smug. "Yes," she bit out.

"Let me speak with him."

She held out the phone. "He wants to talk to you."

Sam rose, taking the receiver. "Jordan," he greeted the older man cheerily, "nice of you to call. Abby was just trying to figure out a way to evict me graciously."

She looked up at him, her eyes widening with surprise. He only grinned in response. "Of course I won't let her get away with it," he assured the man on the other end of the long-distance wire. "Don't worry, I'll keep in touch." He handed the phone back to Abby. "He wants to say good-bye."

"Jordan," Abby tried again, "I honestly appreciate your concern, but—" She listened as he listed all the logical reasons for Sam to remain in the house. "All right," she agreed finally. "But if nothing else happens in one week, the man goes." Her eyes lifted to Sam's, handing him a firm-edged warning. "Goodbye, Jordan."

"Well?" His eyes were smiling as he looked down at her.

"You know very well what happened," she snapped. "He threatened to come home to L.A. if I didn't allow you to stay here. He said I was stuck with one of you, and since he had committee meetings scheduled all week, it would be a lot easier on him if I'd agree to put up with you."

"He cares for you, Abby," Sam pointed out softly. "He doesn't want you hurt."

She sank back down into the chair, pressing her fingertips against her forehead. When she lifted her gaze to his silent, watchful one, her eyes mirrored her distress.

"I still think you two are jumping to conclusions. It's probably all just some contrived scheme to get me married off." She hadn't meant to say that. Abby wished she could recall the words the moment they escaped her lips.

He arched a wry brow. "I don't remember asking you to marry me, Abby. Now who's the one jumping to conclusions?"

She flushed at that, a mixture of embarrassment and anger rising like danger flags in her cheeks. "I don't want you staying here."

"You don't have any choice."

"The hell I don't," she retorted. "You can't just move in like you own the place, Sam Garrett. This is my house and don't you dare forget it!"

"Forget it?" he asked with a harsh laugh. "How could I possibly forget a thing like that? It's *your* house, *your* beach, your Mercedes roadster sitting in the garage, and your damn Fortune 500 company." He waved his hand, encompassing the room, the beach, everything. "It's all yours, isn't it, Abby? Swan Pharmaceuticals, this place, the condo at Aspen? Abby Swan, princess of all she surveys."

His tone was bitter as he leaned toward her, his eyes blazing with fury. "I promised Jordan I was going to watch out for you, lady, and I'm not about to go back on my word. So you're stuck with me, whether you like it or not."

"I don't," Abby snapped, jumping up from the chair and stomping toward the door. "I've got a meeting this morning," she informed him briskly. "As much as I'd love continuing this little chat, I have to go."

"I'm coming with you."

"That's not necessary."

"I'll get my jacket and be right down."

Abby decided that she'd teach Sam Garrett a thing or two. She was more than capable of going to the damn bank without a keeper. Once he was upstairs, she'd simply leave.

"Oh, and if you get any ideas about running off without me, you may find it a bit difficult without these." He dangled her keys from his hand. "I've got the spare set, too," he advised dryly when her gaze slid to the drawer where she usually kept them. "So, unless your private school education included hot-wiring a car, sweetheart, you'll just have to wait for me."

His head just cleared the doorframe as the vase of daisies shattered against the molding.

Her meeting that morning didn't go any better than the one the day before and when they returned again to the beach house, Abby turned into a whirlwind of activity, spending hours on the telephone in a vain attempt to gain funding for her project.

"You need to take a break," Sam said, bringing her a cup of tea that night. She hadn't touched the lunch or dinner he'd placed on the desk. "You can't keep working like this."

"I can't quit, either," she retorted, throwing down her pencil. It hit on the eraser, bouncing across the room.

"Good idea," he said amiably. "Throwing things is a terrific release. Even if you did almost deck me this morning." He picked up a ballpoint pen. "Here," he offered, holding it out to her, "try this."

Abby shook her head. "That's silly."

"Just try it."

"Sam . . ."

His eyes were sparkling with encouragement. "Humor me."

"Oh, all right," she said, taking the pen and flipping it halfheartedly across the room.

"Another." He handed her one from his pocket.

This time Abby didn't protest; she hurled it with a bit more force.

"Now you're getting the idea," Sam said with a grin. "Now this." He held out the heavy green ledger book.

With a perverse sort of pleasure, Abby flung it into a far corner, watching the pages ruffle as it settled. "That felt kind of good," she admitted, picking up a thick dictionary.

Sam had to duck as it almost hit his shoulder, but it finally came skidding to a halt halfway to the large picture window.

"This is fun," she enthused, beginning to throw whatever inanimate objects she could reach. When the floor looked as if World War III had just been fought in her living room, she collapsed onto the couch.

"Thank you, Sam. I needed that."

"You need to relax," he said, holding up a hand to forestall the protest he knew was coming. "I understand the pressures on you right now, Abby. But let's make a deal."

She eyed him suspiciously. "What type of deal? The last time I negotiated with you I agreed to let you stay here for one night. Now you seem to have every intention of settling in for the duration."

He ignored her sarcasm. "You can work as much as you like, but every few hours you take a break and do something just for yourself."

"I don't know—"

"Abby," he said reasonably, "if you work yourself into the ground getting the money, you won't have any energy left to produce the movie."

He was right, she admitted. And it was nice that he really seemed to care about her. Despite his protestations to the contrary, Abby didn't think Sam was as black-hearted as he'd like her to believe. A soft smile displayed her acquiescence.

A truce was forged as Sam and Abby spent the next few days in peaceful cohabitation. It was, Sam considered late one afternoon, as if the relentless tides of the sea wore away her cool restraint along with the golden sands. She began to relax in his presence, she laughed more easily, and each afternoon, without fail, she jogged up the beach to visit with Louie. There was a strong bond between the two of them, he realized, experiencing an odd sense of something akin to jealousy each time she kissed the old man's weatherworn cheek.

He had not forgotten her one-week deadline and wondered what would happen when the time came for him to leave. While he had no intention of abandoning her to whoever was threatening her life, he wasn't looking forward to another altercation.

One afternoon, as they walked down the beach, collecting shells to add to Abby's collection, it had occurred to Sam suddenly that somehow, he and Abby had become friends. With the exception of Mary O'Neill, whom he'd grown up with, Sam had never been friends with a woman before. It came as a surprise how much he was enjoying it.

When he'd first come here, all he could think about was how much he wanted Abby, how he wanted to take her to bed. He still wanted that, but more and more he was considering how much he liked her.

It took a united effort, but they managed to avoid the sensual snare that threatened to settle down around them from time to time, the unspoken agreement remaining in force. When the week passed without a word from Abby, Sam breathed a little easier, knowing he'd been given a reprieve. Two nights later, as they walked up the stairs together, Sam wished things could go on this way forever.

When he stopped outside her room, Abby considered how right it felt to have Sam in the house with her. How important his company had become, how she looked forward to viewing that devastatingly attractive smile each morning. They'd been growing closer together, day by day, and she knew that if Sam pushed the issue, she wouldn't be able to tell him no.

Sam cupped her chin in his fingers and lifted her face for a light, tender kiss that nevertheless left her trembling.

"Sweet dreams," he said, his fingers gently stroking a path up her cheek.

"You, too," she whispered.

Dangerous, she reminded herself. Sam Garrett was dangerous, and if he was right about her accidents, everything about her life was rife with peril. Yet all she could think of at this moment was how those firmly chiseled lips felt against hers.

It was impossible to miss the desire on Abby's soft features and Sam knew that although Abby was willing to make love tonight, it would only complicate matters. She was not the type of woman to give herself lightly; Sam didn't want her seeing promises where none existed. He allowed himself one more lingering kiss, savoring the sweet taste of her lips, reminding himself that this was as far as he could go without getting in over his head.

He reached past her, opening her bedroom door. "Good night."

When Abby didn't move, Sam found himself drowning in her liquid silver gaze.

"Abby," he warned, his voice strained, "if you know what's good for you, you'll tell me to go."

Entranced by his intense gaze, Abby found words an impossibility. She stared up at him, shaken by the raw desire blazing in his eyes. But there was something else as well. A touch of sadness that wrenched at her soul.

She slowly shook her head. "I can't," she whispered. "God help me, Sam, I can't send you away."

He pulled her against him, his fingers tangling in her long black hair as his lips covered hers in a harsh, unrelenting kiss that displayed his frustration with their situation.

"Then God help us both," he grated, his breath harsh against her skin as he carried her into the bedroom. "Because I can't leave you alone, no matter how hard I try."

At his rough tone, Abby's body went rigid. "No," he murmured, lying her on the bed. "Don't be afraid, sweetheart. I won't hurt you." Even as he said it, Sam knew that to be a lie. She would be hurt. What in the hell did he think he was doing?

Her soft smile was his undoing and as she reached up, pressing her hand against his heaving chest, Sam shuddered.

"I'm not afraid," she said. "Not of you, Sam. Never you."

"I've got to be crazy," he groaned, his fingers moving of their own volition at the buttons of her cotton blouse.

"I know the feeling," she whispered, closing her eyes as he folded back the material, exposing the satin of her skin. "Oh, Sam, no one has ever made me feel like this."

Sam's body flamed at her softly issued confession, and he quickly stripped off her blouse and lacy bra, allowing a taste of her creamy flesh. When his lips grazed her swollen breast, Abby gasped, her fingers twining through his hair to press him even closer. When his tongue flicked her distended nipple, she cried out, tugging at his shirt in a desperate attempt to touch him.

His body ached, demanding a quick fulfillment of needs too long denied, but Sam forced himself to go slowly as he concentrated on Abby's pleasure. He returned his lips to hers, kissing her slowly, deeply, hungrily, his tongue sweeping the moist interior of her mouth.

Abby's head reeled as she surrendered to Sam's devastating kiss. Her hands moved over his body, up the tense muscles of his side, around to press against his hard chest, her fingers tangling in the soft hairs she found there. When her touch trailed even lower, Sam thought he'd explode.

He grasped her hands, practically yanking them from his aching body to hold them over her head. Abby blinked, her pupils wide and dilated as she attempted to focus on his face.

"Sam?" she asked hesitantly.

"My control isn't what it should be right now," he admitted, a quirk of a smile twisting his mouth. "I think it might be better if you just let me make love to you for a while."

"But..." Her soft gaze expressed her feelings far more than words ever could, and Sam had to fight from cringing as he viewed the uncensored love shining in her wide gray eyes.

You're a real bastard, Garrett, he told himself, even as he brought her hands to his lips. "Trust me, Abby."

As she met his promising gaze, Abby felt herself melting. Her mouth was suddenly very dry, and as she licked her parched lips and nodded slowly, Sam had to stifle a groan.

He rose to his knees, unbuttoning her white jeans. As he pulled them slowly down her legs, inch by devastating inch, he pressed gentle kisses against her skin. She was trembling, her eyes closed to his tender torment, her lashes a thick black fringe against her pink flushed cheeks.

"You're beautiful," he murmured, his words a soft breeze against the inside of her thighs. "So very, very lovely." When his fingers curled around the lacy waistband of her bikini panties, Abby's hips lifted off the mattress in mute offering.

"Sam," she cried out softly, as the scrap of silk seemed to melt away. "Please..."

"Please what, Abby?" he asked, bending down to nibble at her full lower lip. "Please touch you?" His hands cupped her aching breasts, the pads of his thumbs grazing the rosy crowns. "Here? Do you want me to touch you here?"

"Oh, yes," she whispered, moving fluidly under his intimate caresses, her mind floating sensuously as she gave herself up to these golden feelings created by his skillful hands.

His fingers moved lower, splayed across her rib cage. "And here?" he asked, pressing his hand against her abdomen.

Abby trembled from the circular motions of his broad hands against her skin, the unexpected pleasure-pain as his teeth suddenly nipped her earlobe. Unable to answer, she arched her back, pressing herself against the calloused skin of his palms.

She felt as if she were floating as he lifted her in his arms, turning her over, straddling her body as his lips created a wet, flaming swathe down her back, creating sparks between the delicate bones of her spine. When those strong fingers cupped her rounded buttocks, massaging her soft flesh, Abby moaned into her pillow.

Her bones had turned to water and she offered no resistance when Sam pulled her onto his lap, cradling her against his chest, kissing her lingeringly, lovingly, his questing hand unerringly locating the heated core of her desire.

Through the swirling fog clouding her senses, Abby realized that Sam was still fully dressed. The stiff denim of his jeans scraped against her as she twisted wantonly in his arms and as her hands circled his waist, they had to move under the cotton of his shirt to feel his warm, moist skin. While there was something admittedly erotic about lying naked in the arms of a fully clad man who was doing wonderful, wicked things to her body, Abby was overcome with a sudden shyness.

"No," she moaned, "I can't. Not like this."

His fingers abandoned their warm harbor to slide enticingly up and down her inner thighs and he bent his head, kissing the soft hollow at the base of her throat where her pulse hammered wildly out of control.

"Yes, you can, Abby," he corrected gently. "There aren't any secrets between us, sweetheart. Not tonight. Tonight we can do anything, feel anything." His clever fingers teased at her most sensitive spot, drawing a muffled gasp as she buried her head in his shoulder. "Tell me you don't want this and I'll leave right now."

Unable to lie, Abby felt the tension building deep within her. Her body began to hum like a live wire, thousands of throbbing pulses beating harder, faster. Her breathing was ragged; all her senses were riveted on Sam's arousing touch, his strong, yet infinitely gentle fingers as they kneaded her warm flesh, bringing her to the very edge of insanity.

A rosy film came over her eyes, blinding her to everything but the exquisite liberties Sam was taking with her body. He continued to lead her higher, then higher still, to where the air grew thin and thought disintegrated, replaced by a myriad of sensations: blazing heat, dazzling light, and a swirling blood-red passion that swept her up, carrying her beyond pleasure, beyond ecstasy, to a shimmering distant place, far above any she'd ever been.

Crying out, Abby wrapped her arms about Sam, fusing her mouth to his, their breath mingling as she whispered incoherent words of love.

As much as he'd been hungering for Abby, her uninhibited response tore at some primitive fiber deep inside Sam. When her cries softened to gentle sighs, he slid her off his lap onto the mattress. As he flung off his clothes, Sam's gleaming eyes locked with her own wide, wondrous ones.

Her ebony hair was spread out over the pillow, her eyes held the soft glow of buffed pewter, and her parted lips were dark and swollen from his long, draining kisses. She looked wonderfully, wildly wanton, and as she held out her arms, giving him a soft, inviting smile, Sam felt a surge of need so strong he was afraid to touch her. She was so small, so delicate . . . The last thing he wanted to do was hurt her.

But obsession created its own demands, madness its own power and as he crushed her beneath him, a blazing heat exploded deep within him. Sam wasn't aware of saying her name, over and over as he thrust into her, taking her in a whirlwind of passion. The fire rose, fusing their flesh, searing away reason, the flames scorching away any lingering inhibitions. Sam was overcome by an almost unbearable pain of incomprehensible pleasure that went on, and on, until he thought he'd died. Then everything went dark, and he collapsed on Abby's pliant flesh, his body spent.

He didn't know how long he lay there, his head between her breasts, his long legs tangled with hers, but Sam gradually became aware of her heartbeat as it slowly, inexorably returned to a more normal rhythm. What in the hell had he been thinking of, he groaned inwardly. The passion that had infused his body was replaced by regret, guilt and despair.

Bracing himself for a devastating sense of loss, he slowly withdrew from Abby's soft warmth, rolling over onto his back. Not ready to meet what he knew would be a heartbreakingly tender expression, he flung his arm over his eyes.

Abby lay silently beside him, numbed by Sam's response. She hadn't expected him to declare his undying love. But neither had she expected him to act so coolly. She bit her lip, concentrating on the pain, as she fought back the traitorous tears. When she didn't think she could stand the lingering silence another moment, she cast a cautious glance in his direction.

"Sam?" she whispered into the moonlight-spangled darkness.

His only response was a muffled oath that didn't leave her feeling any better. She propped herself up on one elbow, deciding to try again.

"Sam?" she repeated softly, reaching out, touching his shoulder hesitantly. He flinched, causing tendrils of icy fear to wrap themselves around her heart.

When he finally looked at her, his eyes were dark and bleak in the moonlight streaming through the window. "I didn't mean for that to happen," he said with bitter self-loathing.

"You've been saying all along that you wanted me," she reminded him softly.

He sat up abruptly, swinging his legs over the side of the bed. "Of course I wanted you; what red-blooded male wouldn't?"

Despite his gritty tone, Abby knew it went deeper than that. Sam cared for her. She knew he did. She'd seen it in his eyes.

"Was that all it was? Just a quickie with Jessica Thorne?"

Sam muttered a harsh oath, which Abby knew was directed inward. "Damn it, you know better than that. I wanted you. Not some image created by a group of Hollywood scriptwriters."

"And I wanted you," she argued softly. "So what's the matter?"

"I told you. I don't mix sex and work."

While Abby wanted to point out that what they'd shared had transcended mere sex, she decided this was probably not the time. "But this is different," she said instead. "We're different."

He rose from the bed, picking up his scattered clothes. "That's the problem," he muttered under his breath, headed toward the door.

"Sam—"

He spun on his bare heel, his face unrelenting. But the dark despair in his eyes made Abby want to cry. He took a deep breath and she watched, entranced as his hard chest rose and fell. *Even now,* she thought ruefully. *Even when I'm having the most depressing conversation of my life, I still want him. Still love him.*

"Look, Abby," he said roughly, "this was a mistake." A lightning bolt of pain seared through him as he saw her gentle eyes begin to fill with tears. Forcing his voice to a softer tone, Sam tried again. "Not that it wasn't terrific. It was. You were wonderful and I'd love nothing more than to spend the rest of the night sharing that bed with you."

"I'd like that, too, Sam," Abby said softly.

"Ah, Abby," he said with a sigh, returning to sit on the edge of the bed. His knuckles brushed a familiar path up her cheek. "Sweetheart, don't you see? All that would do is complicate things even more."

"And you don't like complications, do you, Sam?" Abby asked, her eyes searching his for hidden messages.

"I can't afford any." Sam took a deep breath, forcing himself not to give into temptation and kiss those trembling lips. "Get some sleep," he suggested, his fingers giving her another message altogether as they trailed down her throat. "We can talk about this in the morning. Things always look better in the light of day."

Reminding herself that she had to survive this with some dignity, Abby nodded, remaining silent as Sam left the room.

She lay awake all night, unable to stop thinking about Sam. Abby had certainly been kissed before; on *Potomac* she shared scenes with men that women all over the world fantasized making love with. So why had Sam's kiss tilted her world on its axis? Why did his lips, his touch, the way his eyes darkened when he looked at her, surpass anything she'd ever imagined? Abby had not been prepared for the turmoil, the aching need he'd created within her and even now her mind whirled with renewed desire that both intrigued and frightened her.

She knew they'd been working toward this crossroads since the beginning. All too often they'd shared those unexpected flares of desire, but until tonight she'd been able to turn away from the temptation. And when they had made love, it was like nothing she'd ever known. She'd never experienced such a total lack of control, she'd never burned for a man as she had for Sam. As he had for her.

But he had made it perfectly clear that what they'd experienced had been nothing more than a sexual interlude; a lapse that would not be repeated. Abby didn't know how she could continue living under the same roof with Sam without making love to him now that she'd experienced ecstasy in his arms. The thing to do, she decided, was to plan her strategy carefully, keeping their conversation to a few safe topics until Sam was gone.

Politics was definitely out; they'd be bound to begin arguing and past experience had already demonstrated Sam's ability to make her temper flare dangerously out of control. That was the one thing she didn't want to happen. Anger had an unfortunate way of turning into desire all too easily when she was around the man.

Religion was also out, she decided, knowing it to be a dangerous topic at the best of times. There was always the weather, that would be safe enough. But how long could they discuss high fronts and jet streams?

Abby tried to come up with something she and Sam shared in common, which immediately brought their easily sparked attraction to mind. "Nope," she groaned, closing her eyes. "That one definitely won't do."

She might be able to avoid talking about sex, but she couldn't stop her rebellious mind from thinking about it. With her eyes closed, she could envision Sam's lips approaching hers. She could feel his warm breath against her, taste him. She was drowning in deep waves of desire even as her heart ached with a love she knew he'd never accept.

"What on earth am I going to do?" she whispered into the darkness. Then she cried.

9

As Abby entered the kitchen the next morning, Sam handed her a cup of coffee and sat down in the chair across the table. She sipped the steaming coffee in silence, appreciating the fact that Sam never seemed to expect sparkling conversation in the morning. Especially this morning, she considered, wondering how to bring up last night. The dark shadows under his eyes were evidence that Sam had slept as little as she. But she'd already known that; she'd heard him pacing the floor of the small guest bedroom long into the night.

Her gaze drifted outside the kitchen window, taking in the glasslike smoothness of the ocean. "It's a nice day."

"It's supposed to rain tomorrow."

Abby shrugged. "That's okay. I like the rain."

"Me, too."

At his nonchalant tone, Abby congratulated herself on how well this was going. This might work out, after all. She'd probably been exaggerating her fears.

"What do you like to do when it rains?" he asked casually.

"Oh, I love the excuse to do absolutely nothing important. I read, catch up on my favorite soap operas.... What do you like to do?"

Abby knew she'd made a tactical error as she watched the dark desire coalesce in his eyes. "Make love."

"Oh," she whispered. Then she shook her head regretfully. "Well, so much for that one."

He lifted an inquisitive brow. "I'm afraid that reference escapes me."

"I was trying to come up with safe conversational topics," she admitted. "For a minute there, it looked as if we'd be okay discussing the weather. But I guess it's off-limits, too."

"It seems so," Sam agreed. "Did you come up with any other conversational gambits?"

She shook her head, unable to answer. Thought was difficult enough with those oddly tender eyes warming her face; speech was impossible.

"How about I try to come up with one?" he suggested, his dark gaze moving across her face. "I spent all last night wanting you again, Abby."

She turned away, knowing if she continued to look into those molten gold pools of Sam's eyes, she'd surely drown.

"Abby?" His tone was soft, but Abby recognized it for what it was. A command.

"Would you like your coffee warmed up?" she asked suddenly, in a desperate attempt to change the subject. She reached out for his cup, but Sam shook his head in denial.

"The coffee is fine. Abby, we have to talk about it."

Abby swallowed. "That's really not necessary, Sam. After all, I'm a grown woman. I'm not going to get all misty-eyed and mistake a little recreational sex for anything serious."

"Is that all it was?"

She met his surprised gaze with a level one of her own. "Wasn't it?"

He shrugged, believing that for Abby, it had gone far deeper. Realizing she was trying to protect herself from further pain, he decided not to argue.

"I suppose so. What do you suggest we do next?"

"You can always leave," she suggested flatly. "The way we're spending so much time together under the same roof, it was probably inevitable that we'd feel attracted to each another."

"That's a possibility," he agreed. "As a matter of fact, I am leaving. Today."

Abby closed her eyes briefly to the stab of pain caused by his words. "You are?"

"I called downtown to see how things were coming along on that stationery lead. They've picked up the guy who wrote you those letters, Abby. You're out of danger. There's no reason for me to stay around any longer."

Abby attempted to keep an even tone. "I guess not."

Play it light, Sam warned himself. He reached across the table, lifting her downcast chin with his finger. "Hey, this is good news."

Abby attempted a smile that died on her trembling lips. "Yes. It is, isn't it?"

Unable to sit still, she left the table, wandering over to stare out the window. The sun was shining. The tide was going out, as it had since the beginning of time. Dolphins were frolicking in the deep blue waters and an old beachcomber roamed the sand, picking up glistening shells left behind by the outrushing tide. Life was continuing as if nothing had happened. As if Sam wasn't leaving.

Sam watched her silently, wondering what kind of bastard he was that he hadn't celebrated when he'd gotten the word this morning. He didn't want Abby's life to be in danger; he couldn't bear the thought of anything happening to her. But he was going to miss her. Miss her very badly.

Abby turned around, appearing more vulnerable than usual. "I don't suppose we'll be seeing each other again," she said, her voice going up a little on the end of the statement, turning it into a question.

"Hey, sure," he lied. "We'll get together and talk about old times."

"We don't have any old times," she pointed out.

He'd known he had no business getting mixed up with Abby Swan. She was looking for a relationship where none could exist. Hell, anything between them would have about as much substance as a sand castle.

"Sure we do," he argued enthusiastically. "We've got those walks on the beach, chili dogs, Louie."

Her teeth bit into her lower lip. "Louie's going to miss you."

"He'll have you."

"Yes. Well..." She took a deep breath, gathering courage to ask the next question. "What about us, Sam?"

Sam shook his head. "Abby—"

She held her ground. "I'm not going to believe that you don't care about me."

"Of course I do, Abby. We all care. Jordan, Johnny—"

"Damn it, that's not what I mean and you know it!" she shouted, surprising both of them with her display of emotion.

Sam stared at her for a long, silent moment. Then he walked over to her, tucking her hair behind her ears, framing her face with his palms.

"You're a very special lady, Abby. Given other circumstances, who knows what might have happened.... But I'm a realist and there's no way you can convince me that we'd survive two weeks together. We're too different to make it work."

Abby felt no shame as her eyes pleaded with him to understand. "Haven't you ever heard about opposites attracting?"

"That's a nice little textbook theory, but in real life it just doesn't wash, honey." Sam told himself that he couldn't allow Abby any false hope. He'd hurt her enough as it was. "Besides, if you want the unvarnished truth, you're not my type."

Abby was stunned at how much those words stung. "Exactly what kind of woman am I?" she asked, despite her better judgment.

"The forever-after type," Sam answered without hesitation.

"Is that so bad?" she asked softly.

"I knew last night was a mistake," Sam muttered under his breath.

Abby refused to be deterred. She knew Sam cared for her far more than he was admitting. Every look, every touch, every kiss had proclaimed his feelings more than words ever could. She took a deep breath and plunged into untested waters.

"Look, Sam, you want a no-strings affair? You've got it. Do you see me professing undying love? Am I asking you to marry me? And I certainly don't remember fighting you off last night. So what's the problem?"

Sam mumbled a response.

"I didn't quite catch that," she invited with far more aplomb than she was feeling. Sam was obviously more determined than she'd first thought and Abby was beginning to feel as if she had leaped in over her head.

"You're rich, damn it!" he shouted.

Knowing how he felt about her money, Abby felt the last vestiges of hope slipping away. "We're back to that."

"There doesn't seem to be any escaping it," he agreed grimly. He shook his head, then turned away. "I'd better go pack."

Abby could not let it end like this. "Sam?"

He turned in the doorway, fighting down a rebellious surge of desire. And something else he couldn't put his finger on. "Yeah, Abby?"

She swallowed, trying to force the words past the painful lump in her throat. "Thanks. Thanks for everything."

"It's my job," he said gruffly, unreasonably pained by the sheen in her gray eyes. Dragging his gaze away, he took the stairs two at a time, vowing to get out of this house before he said something he didn't mean.

THE THIRD DAY after Sam's departure, Kate showed up at the beach house with some papers for Abby to sign. "Where's the hunk?" she asked, the minute Abby opened the door.

"Who knows?" Abby replied with feigned nonchalance.

"From the way those sexy gold eyes were eating you up, I expected to find him all settled in for the duration." As much at home here as in her own house in Santa Monica, Kate went immediately to the kitchen, opening the refrigerator. "What's for lunch?"

"If you want to eat here, I think you're stuck with chili dogs," Abby advised. "I haven't been shopping."

Kate pulled her head out of the refrigerator, eyeing Abby judiciously. "You haven't been sleeping, either," she diagnosed, taking in the dark shadows under Abby's lackluster eyes. "I take it this has something to do with Sam Garrett, FBI?"

"It doesn't have a thing to do with him," Abby denied firmly. "I'm just worried about the funding for *Medicine Woman*. If I don't come up with something pretty soon, my option will run out." She took a deep, frustrated breath. "And on top of that, Walter Mann is waiting to grab the thing up."

"Mann?" Kate groaned. "Oh God, Abby, you can't let him do that! He'll make the heroine a physician at a teenage

boys' camp and have her playing doctor with all the campers."

"While a deranged ax-murderer, who just happens to be
the jealous teenage daughter of the former camp doctor, is
running around chopping up the place," Abby tacked on.

The two women eyed each other with very real depression.

"You don't really think he's going to get his hands on it,
do you?" Kate asked.

"Do you happen to have twenty million dollars on you?"

"Let me check," her friend answered, pulling out a worn
leather billfold. She placed the bills on the table. "Twelve
dollars and forty-seven . . . -eight . . . fifty cents."

"We're a bit short."

"A tad," Kate admitted. "Ever think of selling your
body?"

Abby arched a dark brow. "In this town? With all the
freebies running around, who'd ever pay?"

"You've got a point. Although, Jessica Thorne might pull
a pretty penny."

"Even if I'd consider that—which I won't—" Abby
warned, "can you imagine what kind of performance you'd
have to give for twenty million dollars?"

"It'd be easier just to marry some rich old coot," Kate
considered, chewing on a long red fingernail. "Of course,
speaking of old coots, there's always some of that lovely
Matthew Swan money you're so dead set against touching."

"I won't use my father's money," Abby said tightly, her
eyes handing Kate a hard-edged warning the woman had
seen before.

"Then you'd better get used to the idea of your *Medicine
Woman* wearing a sexy white miniskirt, because she's going

to be Walter Mann's pretty soon," Kate remarked briskly. "This place is getting depressing; let's go out for lunch."

"I'm not dressed," Abby protested, not wanting to leave. What if Sam called? What if he wanted her to come down to headquarters and identify someone? Or make a statement? Or whatever one did at the FBI.

"You look fine. Come on. I'm dying for a guacamole salad."

"I don't know."

Abby hated her atypical vacillation. She'd been like this since Sam had forged his way into her life, and if she had thought things would get better once he'd gone, she was sadly mistaken. He'd left a void that was impossible to fill. As desperate as she was about her funding problem, as irritating as the constant calls from her agent had been about signing a new contract for *Potomac*, as worrisome as were Ken's continued problems with the board of directors of Swan Pharmaceuticals, nothing had managed to drive Sam Garrett from her mind. She thought about him constantly, knowing that if he suddenly did answer her wish and show up at the door, she wouldn't have the slightest idea what to say to him.

Before Kate could argue her point the phone rang and Abby literally dove toward it. "Hello?"

Kate's eyes narrowed at the blatant hope in her friend's tone. Abby's breathless answer was followed by a low, flat greeting.

"Oh. Hi, Ken."

She sighed, staring out the window, watching a pair of lovers strolling hand-in-hand down the beach. Why couldn't that be Sam and her? Why did life have to be so complicated? Why did she have to fall in love with a man who considered her only another assignment?

"What?" she asked blankly, dragging her attention back to Ken's rapid-fire conversation. "Yes, I'll be at the board meeting. Yes, I'll back you. I always do, don't I?" She nodded absently. "Of course, Ken. Look, can we talk about this later? I was just on the way out the door.... Lunch," she answered his question. "With Kate, why?"

Kate was gesturing toward the door with one hand, rubbing her stomach with the other as she tried to hurry up Abby's conversation.

"No, I haven't seen Sam since they wrapped up the case. No, he hasn't called." She shook her head wordlessly, trying to regain control of her voice. "No, I don't expect him to. I know you didn't trust him, but he really was a nice man. Honest."

Abby could tell Ken wasn't buying that one as he started in with an entire list of complaints. "Well, it doesn't really matter now, does it?" she broke into his aggravated litany. "The man is gone. Out of our lives ... Ken, I've really got to go." She hung up, staring at the telephone.

"Haven't you ever heard the old adage about a watched phone never ringing?" Kate asked with false brightness. "Come on, do you want the guy to know you're mooning around waiting for him to call? Let your answering machine pick it up."

"Am I that transparent?" Abby asked as they made their way out to the car.

Kate's narrow-eyed gaze swept over Abby's slender frame. "You've lost at least five pounds, you have bags under your eyes Bela Lugosi would envy, and unless you shape up, your contract negotiations will be a moot point. Because they want Jessica Thorne to show up on the first day of shooting, not the bride of Frankenstein."

"It's so nice to have friends," Abby muttered, throwing herself into Kate's Volkswagen Rabbit convertible.

"I've always thought friends were supposed to be straight shooters," Kate returned blandly as she pulled out of the driveway. "Look, if the guy hasn't called you, why don't you quit hovering over that phone, pick it up and call him? This is the eighties, kiddo. Women can actually do that in these enlightened days."

"I can't."

"Why not?"

"What if he doesn't want to talk to me?"

Kate's heavy sigh feathered her auburn bangs. "You sound like my daughter. We went through hell around the house before the last Sadie Hawkin's Day dance. I thought I'd become a raving maniac before she worked up the nerve to call Dennis Wagner."

"Did he accept?" Abby asked with interest.

"Yep."

"Oh."

"Call him, Abby," Kate advised.

"I'll think about it," Abby stated slowly.

Kate grinned, returning her attention to her driving. They drove in comfortable silence, Kate remaining silent, allowing Abby to consider the idea of making the first move.

Abby's mind came up with and immediately discarded several possible ploys. She could never just pick up the phone and say "Hi, Sam, I miss you. How about dropping by for a walk on the beach? And oh, by the way, why don't you pack your toothbrush? So you can spend the night."

Did women really do that, she wondered. Jessica would do it. She knew she would. But Abby wasn't Jessica Thorne and never could be.

"This place has great service," Kate's voice broke into Abby's troubled thoughts. "But I don't think they'll deliver your lunch out here. You have to go in and get it."

Abby looked around, surprised to find herself in the parking lot of Kate's favorite Mexican restaurant. She managed to smile an apology for her inattention, blinking as they entered the dark dining room.

"I love the food here," Kate enthused after the waiter had brought a pitcher of margaritas. "It's one of the few places in town that doesn't put green food coloring in the guacamole."

She ignored Abby's protests, filling two salt-rimmed glasses. "To success," she proclaimed, lifting her glass. "May Abby Swan end up with *Medicine Woman* and Sam Garrett both." She grinned. "I just adore happy endings."

Abby lifted the glass momentarily to her lips, then put it down again, running her finger up and down the stem. "Have you ever asked a man out?"

"Sure," Kate answered blithely. "If we divorced ladies waited for some guys to make the first move, we'd never get out. Some of them actually seem to expect it."

"I don't know," Abby mused. "Sam seems a little old-fashioned."

"All the more reason to shake him up a little," Kate reasoned.

"Perhaps."

It still seemed a little risky. Abby had the distinct impression that Sam liked to be the one in charge. And although his built-in arrogance had admittedly grated on her nerves from time to time, she didn't want to chase him away. Not that she had him, by any wild stretch of the imagination.

She hadn't wanted to love Sam. She'd fought against it from the beginning. She didn't want to walk on the beach, remembering how nice his arm had felt around her shoulders. She didn't want to remember how the lines at the corners of his eyes crinkled when he laughed, and she had tried her best to forget how just the sight of him in the morning was more stimulating than her first cup of coffee had ever been. Abby didn't want to think about Sam every minute of every waking hour, only to have him haunt her dreams. *But you can't always get everything you want*, she reminded herself.

"Aren't you going to eat anything?" Kate was eyeing Abby's untouched plate with disapproval.

Abby stared at it, unable to remember ordering the combination plate. "I'm not really very hungry."

The waiter appeared, a worried frown on his brow. "Is something wrong?"

"Not at all." She managed an encouraging smile. "I'm just not as hungry as I thought."

"Would you like me to box it up so you can take it home for later?"

Abby shook her head, finding the gesture a major effort. "No, thanks. I don't think I'll be very hungry later, either."

"I think you hurt his feelings," Kate observed as they drove back up the coastal highway.

"I autographed that menu for him," Abby pointed out.

"But he wanted to feed you."

"Everyone wants to feed me," she complained. "Some waiter I've never met before, you, Louie, Sam..." Her voice broke on his name and Abby closed her eyes against the pain it caused.

"Got it rough, huh?" Kate murmured sympathetically.

"I don't want to talk about it," Abby stated firmly.

"Sure." Both women remained quiet the rest of the way to the beach house, but as Abby went to exit the car, Kate reached out and touched her arm. "Call the guy, Abby," she advised. "You sure as hell can't feel any worse."

Abby silently agreed as she entered the too lonely house. She would call Sam, she vowed. She'd just casually ask if the investigation was finished and mention that she had tickets to the Dodgers' game. She'd call him. As soon as she checked her messages.

Hello, this is Abby Swan. I'm not home right now, but if you leave your message at the tone, I'll get back to you as soon as I can.

BEEP. "Hiya, Abby, good news. I got a call from the studio; they've gone up two thou an episode. As your agent, I gotta tell you, girl, you'll be making one helluva mistake if you don't get your little butt down here and sign on the dotted line. Call me."

BEEP. "Hey, sweetheart, this is your big brother again. How'd you like to go sailing this weekend? If the weather clears up, that is. Call me."

BEEP. "Abby?" Her heart beat against her ribs as she heard Sam's husky voice. "Damn, I hate these things...." Abby could practically see him thrusting his fingers through his hair. "Look, we need to talk. Can you come by the office tomorrow around ten? I'll be expecting you, unless I hear differently, okay? Well...that's about it." She could tell he was more than a little uncomfortable. "See you tomorrow."

"Tomorrow," she repeated softly, rewinding the tape. "Tomorrow." She began to dance around the room, spinning circles until she became dizzy. Then, oblivious to the slanting rain, she ran down the beach to where Louie was hunkered under a broad red-and-white-striped umbrella.

"Louie! Isn't it an absolutely marvelous day?" she asked, flinging her arms about the old man and dancing around in a little circle with him.

"It's raining," he pointed out. "It's been raining for three days. Do you know what that does to my business?"

"Don't worry, the sun's coming out tomorrow," she promised.

"So what is she now, a weather-lady?"

"Trust me, Louie. Everything's going to be wonderful tomorrow."

His blue eyes narrowed. "Sam is coming back."

"Yes," she said softly, nodding her head, as if even now she was having trouble believing it herself. "Yes," she stated more firmly. "Sam is coming back and the sun will shine and you'll have customers lined up all the way down the beach."

"Crazy," he muttered.

"And hungry," she realized aloud. "Make it two chili dogs, Louie. I'm suddenly starving!"

SAM FOUND HIMSELF WAITING for Abby's arrival with an uncommon impatience. He knew he'd been less than benevolent since returning to work, barking at anything or anyone. But he'd attributed that to normal adjustments to this desk job. However, since his ill temper increased as the time neared for Abby to show up at his office, he was forced to consider that her presence—or more precisely, lack of presence—had something to do with the fact he'd been roaring about the place like a wounded lion.

It wasn't extraordinary that he couldn't stop thinking about her, he assured himself. After all, he was closing up her case. Her name appeared on numerous pieces of paper crossing his desk. She was business. Strictly business.

If that's so, Sam mused, glaring out at the rain streaked windows, why did she fill his mind when he went home? Why couldn't he even forget her long enough to get some sleep? She was always with him—her throaty laugh, her wide gray eyes that turned so quickly to molten silver, the way she talked with her hands, moving them like graceful birds whenever she spoke. It had been those slender hands that had given Sam the notion she was not nearly so self-contained as she tried to appear. He couldn't forget how they'd felt on his flesh, roaming his body with gentle, yet uninhibited touches.

Abby Swan had been nothing but a woman in trouble, a case he'd taken on as a favor for a friend. She had no right to infiltrate herself into his mind this way. His scowling gaze moved to the clock on the wall. What was the matter with it this morning? It read only two minutes later than the last time he checked.

Finally, his intercom buzzed, announcing her arrival, and he rose from his desk, taking his jacket down from the coatrack. The polite, official response he'd planned fled his mind as she opened the door.

"Abby."

He couldn't help staring; she was so breathtakingly lovely. Her eyes were glowing, her color was bright, her smile warm. Her hair cascaded over her shoulders, waves of ebony satin, and she exuded a heady, provocative scent. Sam suddenly felt like a parched man coming across a sparkling oasis in the desert and as he drank in her beauty, desire rose within him in heated waves.

"Sam," she answered simply, her eyes betraying her feelings better than words ever could.

He'd never wanted anyone more in his life, never needed a woman like he needed Abby Swan. He slipped his hands into his pockets, not trusting himself to shake her hand. If he touched her, his resolve would disappear.

"Come in," he said, turning away, anxious to put the wide expanse of desk between them. He needed a physical barrier to help him maintain the more vital emotional one.

Abby watched, a puzzled frown furrowing her brow. What was the matter with him? He'd invited her here today, yet he didn't seem all that pleased to see her.

She was still standing in the doorway, appearing hesitant and damn it, Sam considered, vulnerable. He hated it when she looked like that. It pulled unwelcome chords deep within him. It increased his need to hold her even more.

"Why don't you sit down?" He gestured at a chair on the other side of his desk.

Abby's fingers tightened about her fawn clutch bag until her knuckles turned white. *A mistake*, she realized belatedly. *This is all a horrible mistake.*

"Will this take long?" she asked, feeling an almost desperate need to escape his calm scrutiny. She couldn't allow him to know how much his message had meant to her. "I've, uh, got a lunch date," she lied.

"I'll be as brief as possible."

"Thank you."

As she made her way across the room, Sam surveyed the slender body that haunted his sleep. She was wearing that ivory silk suit again, but if memory served him correctly, it had fit differently a week ago. He could remember it caressing her curves, today it appeared to be hanging on her. And were those shadows under her eyes?

"I called you in because we've got a slight glitch in our program," he stated in a distant, official tone.

"A glitch?"

"I told you they picked up the guy writing you those letters."

Abby nodded. "Yes. That was right before you left." Her eyes darkened with something that appeared to be an accusation.

"Yes. Well, something's come up." Her expression didn't alter, she didn't question him, the only sign she'd heard him at all was the tightening of her fingers in her lap. "Hell, Abby," Sam said with an exasperated breath, "he'll only admit to one."

Her expression revealed her confusion. "One?"

"One."

"But I received at least six over the past few months."

"Eight," Sam confirmed. "But the guy swears he only wrote you the first one."

"That doesn't make sense," she argued.

"I'll be the first to agree with that."

She sighed, watching the silver raindrops stream down the window. So much for a sunny tomorrow. If Sam was any more remote, he'd be accusing her of writing the letters herself and taking her downstairs and fingerprinting her or booking her, or whatever it was people did in places like this.

Sam fought the urge to go to her. There was so much he wanted to say, so many things he wanted to offer her. But he was not one to deal in self-delusion and Sam knew that he had nothing at all to offer a woman like Abby Swan. They were light-years apart and always would be.

"So," she said finally, returning a steady gray gaze his way. "What now?"

"For now, nothing. We're rechecking the later letters for any fingerprints we might have missed, just in case the guy's telling the truth. But to be honest, I don't expect to find anything new there."

"I see. So what you're telling me is, the later letters might be merely a coincidence?"

"I'm not sure," he hedged.

"What do I do now?" she asked sharply. "Go home and wait to see if some lunatic shows up at my kitchen door?"

"You don't have to worry about that; I've put you under constant surveillance."

"I haven't seen anyone."

He brushed off her words with a brusque wave of his hand. "If our agents were that obvious, they wouldn't be effective."

Something else occurred to her. "Did you say *you* had men watching me?"

He nodded.

"I see," she murmured. "I had no idea that you were so important around here, Sam. I suppose I should feel flattered that I received such *personal* attention from the boss man himself."

"I told you I was taking a desk job," he reminded her.

Her cool gray gaze raked over him. "That's right, you did. What's the matter, are you too busy behind your important desk these days to handle the dirty work yourself?"

"Damn it, Abby, that's not it at all. Besides, we both know what would happen if I moved back in with you."

"You're taking an awful lot for granted, aren't you?" she countered, secretly admitting Sam was right.

Knowing there was no point in arguing further, Sam resisted the temptation to say that the chemistry between them was as strong as ever. Stronger, if that was possible. There was no way he and Abby could ever maintain a platonic relationship.

"Believe me, Abby, the agents watching you are the best we've got. You're well protected."

"You've no idea how secure that makes me feel," she ground out, her tone heavily laced with sarcasm.

"You weren't so worried about your safety last week," Sam countered, becoming more and more frustrated by her unfriendly attitude. "If I recall correctly, you believed Jordan and I were merely exaggerating the potential for danger."

"Last week was last week," she tossed back. "Things are different now."

"What things?" he demanded, his palms pressing against the polished mahogany top of the desk as he leaned toward her.

She rose stiffly from the chair, thrusting out her jaw, determined that Sam Garrett would not see her cry. "Things," she replied simply. "Well, if that's all you wanted, Sam, I should be going. I don't want to be late for my lunch date."

Incensed by her cool tone of dismissal, Sam was around the desk in two seconds flat, his fingers curling over her shoulders. "What things are different?" he demanded, looking down into her icy eyes. Frustrated by the way she was retreating from him, hiding behind a high, unbreachable wall of restraint, he shook her. "Damn it, Abby, how are things different than they were last week?"

"You!" she exploded, jerking away, headed for the door.

He caught her by the wrist, spinning her toward him. "What do you mean by that?" Confusion and annoyance made his tone harsh.

She glared down at his fingers braceleting both her wrists. "Let go of me."

"Not until I get an answer."

She shook her head furiously, unwilling to allow Sam to see how badly he had hurt her. So she'd been nothing but an assignment taken on for an old friend. Abby could learn to live with that. What she couldn't bear Sam knowing was that she'd mistaken his professional concern for caring.

"I don't know what I mean," she murmured, biting her lip. Her eyes were veiled as she met his confused gaze.

"Abby, if it's about the other night . . . If anything happens, I hope you'll let me know."

Abby stared at him. If anything happened? How could he be so blind? Of course something had happened. She'd fallen in love with him, opened her entire life to him, only to be tossed aside when her case was closed. If it hadn't been for the problem with the letters, she never would have heard from him again.

"Don't worry, Sam," she said stiffly, looking past him at the presidential painting on his office wall. "I'm not into trapping men with unwanted pregnancies."

His fingers tightened about her wrists. "Abby, I'm trying to do the decent thing here."

In her pain, Abby sought for something to say that would hurt Sam. To make him feel as miserable as she'd been feeling. "I'd say your chivalrous attitude comes a little late, Sam. The time to think of that was before you went to bed with me."

Her words hit too close to home and Sam dragged his gaze from her accusing one, trying to think of something, anything, he could do to make everything up to her. His mind came up blank and he could only shake his head with a very real regret.

"Please, Sam," she requested softly. "Please let me go."

Sam slowly released her, cursing himself as he realized he was actually going to allow her to leave. He reached into his inside jacket pocket, pulling out a card.

"Keep this with you," he instructed tersely. Pulling a pen from his shirt pocket, he scribbled a number on the back. "I've written down my home phone number. If you need anything, you'll be able to reach me at either of those numbers. Anytime, night or day."

Night or day, Abby considered, slightly bemused as she stared at the piece of pasteboard Sam was holding out to her. She could call him any time and he'd come running. Just like she'd done today. All it had taken was a single telephone call to get her rushing down here. The only difference was she'd come out of love, while Sam would come to her only out of duty.

Her fingers were steady but ice-cold as she took the card and calmly tore it in half, then in half again. She dropped the pieces onto the carpet and when she lifted her eyes again to his, they were filled with anger.

"Damn you," she whispered harshly. Then she turned, leaving him standing in the center of his newly furnished office, staring after her.

10

IT RAINED FOR ANOTHER WEEK, making a liar of the lyricist who professed it never rains in California. In truth, Abby didn't mind the rain; it matched her own dejected mood. She seemed to lack the energy to do anything and the rain gave her the excuse to remain indoors, watching the gray clouds hovering over a dark, windswept sea.

More than once she'd picked up the phone, intent on calling Sam. But what could she say that wouldn't reveal her need just to hear the reassuring sound of his deep voice? She found herself hoping for another letter; that at least would give her an excuse to call him.

Jordan Winston fit a weekend visit into his congressional schedule, but Abby begged off his dinner invitation, inventing a slight cold. Jordan revealed that he talked with Sam daily, assuring her that everything was being done to ensure her safety. Abby tried to keep her mind on the conversation, making what she hoped were appropriate statements at the proper intervals, but she could only think of Sam.

She couldn't stop remembering his smile, the gleam of his eyes, the crisp wave of his dark chestnut hair. How she missed him! Abby was stunned at the depth of her need. She'd imagined it possible for one person to infiltrate every corner of her mind, every pore of her body.

She took long, solitary walks along the beach, mindless of the steady drizzle, noting vaguely that Louie had given up on the weather and closed his hot dog stand. She was glad he'd chosen to remain indoors; he was, after all, not a young man. But she missed his wide smile, his steadfast support.

He'd always been there for her. Louie had always represented a source of strength, her rock, and she could have benefited from his presence during the long days of grieving. And she *was* mourning Sam's departure from her life, she realized, staring out at the white crested waves. Her sorrow would have been no less real if he'd actually died.

On the eighth day of her self-imposed exile, Abby woke to a pale sun peeking through the slit in her curtains, realizing that for the first time since Sam had left, she'd slept the entire night through. That, in itself, was herculean progress. She was getting over him, she decided. Her pain had run its course and it was time to get on with her life. She climbed out of bed, going into the bathroom where she took a long shower, scrubbing harshly at her skin, as if to wash off the last vestiges of Sam Garrett. She was a survivor, she reminded herself as she dressed. It was time to get on with living.

As Abby dressed for the board meeting at Swan Pharmaceuticals, she frowned at her reflection, noting that she was either going to have to start eating, or take all her clothes in for tailoring. Her weight loss was immediately evident as she turned, eyeing the skirt that refused to stay up around her waist. Pulling a wide, leather belt from her closet, she wrapped it about herself, cinching in the baggy suit. Today, she vowed, she was going to eat.

Though Abby would have liked to disassociate herself with Swan Pharmaceuticals, the actual extent of her power was displayed in the way everyone snapped to attention the moment she walked in the door. She made a point of dropping in to visit all the vice-presidents, and from the way none of them seemed surprised to see her, she realized the grapevine was working overtime. Word of her appearance preceded her all the way to the fortieth floor where Ken had moved into Matthew Swan's luxurious executive suite.

"Abby!" His blue eyes lit up with warm welcome as he flung open the door and she was immediately wrapped in a hard, brotherly embrace. "Am I ever glad to see you."

"I can imagine," she murmured, lightly extracting herself and taking a seat on the wide leather sofa. She extended her arm along the top. "The natives are restless," she observed casually.

"They've been fighting me at every turn," he admitted, sounding frustrated. Then he gave her a wide, guileless smile. "But now that you're here, perhaps that will stop."

Her fingernail traced small, thoughtful circles on the smooth leather. "I dropped in on Brent Harrison," she stated quietly, naming the most senior of the company's vice-presidents.

"Harrison," Ken muttered. "He's never gotten over the fact that you appointed me and not him as president."

"I think you're exaggerating," she answered, wondering how to bring up Brent's complaints without making her brother think she had turned against him.

Ken shrugged. "Well, whatever, the guy has been on my case since the day I moved in here."

Abby reminded herself how difficult it must have been for Ken to have come from outside, immediately garnering top spot. Her father had set a tradition of promoting from within, and she'd known it was going to ruffle a few feathers when she sought to override Matthew Swan's will and give Ken his birthright. However, what she had seen and heard downstairs represented much more than ruffled feathers.

"It can't have been easy on you," she began carefully.

"I'm used to hard times, Abby," he said significantly, reminding her that his life had been no bed of roses after her father had divorced his mother.

While Betty Swan had found a position working as a secretary to a San Francisco law firm, she'd never remarried, and money had always been tight around their modest home. Ken, Abby had learned from the private investigator, had gone to Cornell on a scholarship, later earning an advanced degree from Harvard. It had been his initiative, as much as his family ties that had earned him the president's office.

"I know, Ken. But I've tried to make that up to you," she stated quietly.

His eyes gleamed with a victorious light as they roamed the expanse of the top floor suite. "You have, Abby," he assured her. "In spades. Now all I need is for you to toss a little of that chairman-of-the-board weight around in today's meeting."

"Speaking of the meeting, I noticed presidential expenditures are on the agenda," she mentioned, treading softly into dangerous territory.

"You have to spend money to make money, Abby. Surely our beloved daddy taught you that."

Abby ignored Ken's sarcasm toward their father. "I think you should have talked it over with me before ordering that corporate jet. Swan personnel have always flown commercial."

"It wastes time. This way I'll be able to fly into a city, get my business done and return sooner, without worrying about airline schedules."

"That's another thing. You've taken a lot of trips, Ken."

"Research and development," he answered without hesitation. "We don't work in a vacuum, Abby. It's good to keep up with what other companies are doing. Besides, we hired some great people away from other places in the past nine months. Their contributions will more than pay for any travel costs."

"That's probably true," she admitted. Even Brent had said the labs had never been better staffed. "But the boat is going to cause problems."

"It's not a boat, it's a yacht, Abby. The *Yankee Princess* is the best racing yacht in the world today."

Abby knew Ken's obsession was sailing; the first thing he'd purchased with his newfound wealth was the sleek sailboat he'd named the *Black Swan*, referring to his own status in the Swan family. While she was sure he knew what he was talking about when stating this new racing yacht's qualifications, Abby had been uncomfortably surprised when Brent Harrison had brought up Ken's latest toy.

"I'm sure it is," she agreed. "But why do we need it?"

"It's good public relations." He leaned forward, his eyes bright. "I've rounded up a terrific crew. Think what it'll do for Swan's image when we bring the America's Cup back to this country. Don't forget, image is everything," he said, stating the tenet she'd heard far too many times living in Los Angeles. "It's high time we updated Swan's."

"I always felt we earned our image with a superior line of pharmaceuticals," Abby felt obliged to argue.

Ken sighed, shaking his head with frustration. "You sound just like Harrison."

"He was my, our," she corrected herself, "father's right-hand man for over thirty-five years."

"And he was good at his job," Ken agreed. "For the time. But things have changed, Abby. Harrison's still in the Dark Ages. If you let him have his way, he'll run the place into the ground."

"I understand your enthusiasm," Abby said slowly. "And you know I appreciate all you've done." She smiled a soft, coaxing smile. "Just do me a favor and go a little slower, all right? Give everyone time to adjust to all the changes."

Ken stiffened, his gaze turning hard. "Does that mean you won't support me in the meeting?"

"I'll always be in your corner, Ken," she answered. "That's what families are all about."

He perched on the edge of the desk, crossing his arms over his chest. "And you won't be proved wrong, honey. When the stockholders see how our profits have soared since adding the generics to our line, sales of Swan Pharmaceuticals stock will set Wall Street records. Everyone will have to fall into line."

Abby returned the warm smile, knowing that Ken's insistence on the generic drugs had proved a gold mine. From the day he'd taken over the management of her father's company, he'd displayed a Midas touch for marketing even Matthew Swan would have envied.

"I'm relieved to hear that," she admitted. "I've had enough worries without having to face a mutiny over here."

His smile faded as his expression revealed concern. "I thought they'd caught the guy writing you those letters."

"Oh, that. Yes, it seems they have."

Since she hadn't heard from Sam, Abby had decided he'd wrapped up the case and seen no reason to contact her. She had thought he might have given her a call, just to ensure she wouldn't be jumping at shadows, but obviously that idea hadn't occurred to him. At any rate, Abby saw no reason to tell Ken about the suspect's initial statement that he'd only written a single letter. Her misguided fan had probably been hoping he'd be in less trouble if he'd written only one.

"Then it must be *Medicine Woman*," Ken offered solicitously.

Abby's shoulders drooped. "I don't think I'm going to make it," she admitted.

Ken slid off the desk, coming to squat in front of her, taking both her hands in his. "Honey, why don't you stop cutting off your nose to spite your face?"

"I don't know what you mean," she lied.

"You could get the funding if you played the game the way the big boys do."

"By using the company."

"Why not?" he asked reasonably.

"I'm not using my father's money to make this film, Ken. It's important that I prove myself in my world, the same way you're proving your value here. Believe me, I'll go ahead and allow my heroine to seduce campers, rather than take one cent from Swan Pharmaceuticals."

His expression betrayed confusion. "Campers? I don't remember any campers in that book."

Abby managed a genuine laugh as she stood up. "It's a long story," she stated. "I'll tell you someday when I get good and drunk."

"I've never seen you drink more than a couple glasses of wine," he replied, rising to his feet as well. His eyes roved her face, as if seeing her hollowed cheeks and shadowed eyes for the first time. "Abby?" he asked gently, "are you sure everything's all right?"

Her smile wobbled a bit, but she resolutely kept it glued to her face. "Fine," she insisted. "Absolutely fine," she repeated with increased vigor. She went up on her toes, kissing his cheek. "We'd better get to that meeting before they lock us out." She was almost to the door when she remembered something. "By the way, how's Kristin?"

"Kristin's out," he admitted with a sheepish grin.

Abby shook her head with mock censure. "I need a score card to keep up with you. Who's the latest blonde to be draping her leggy frame over the penthouse furniture?"

"I seem to be between ladies at the moment." He grinned. "So, how about my favorite lady coming sailing with me tomorrow? You could use some color in those cheeks."

Remembering her vow to get on with her life, Abby nodded. She hadn't been out sailing with Ken in his beloved *Black Swan* for ages.

"I'd like that. What time?"

"Noon?"

"You're on."

Ken gave her a wide smile as he rubbed his hands together. "Terrific. I've been without my best first mate for too long."

The board meeting did nothing to lift Abby's spirits. She struggled for compromise, and felt, as she left the meeting, that for the most part she'd succeeded. Still, she hadn't missed Ken's barely restrained anger when she had been forced to veto both the jet and the racing yacht.

It had begun to rain again and as Abby left the building, she frowned up at the sky. That meant Louie wouldn't be working. She would have liked to talk to him—about the film, Sam, Ken, sailing ships and sealing wax and cabbages and kings. It never mattered what she said to Louie, or what he said to her. She always felt better after one of their conversations.

While Abby struggled at her meeting, Sam was fighting his own battles across town. He spent the afternoon pacing the carpeted floor of his office, as he had for days, unable to get Abby Swan out of his mind. *It's this case*, he told himself. *I've got my reputation to protect, and it won't look good if some lunatic kills America's favorite bitch.* Adding to his worries were memories of that final taping, due to air in a few days. What if the guy they'd picked up really hadn't written those later letters? Would seeing Jessica Thorne blown away in living color trigger the real thing?

As valid as all those reasons were, Sam knew that Abby was tormenting his mind for far different reasons. He'd fallen for her, fallen hard, and it was only the knowledge that nothing could ever come of an affair with her that kept him from going over there and taking her to bed. That fantasy had blossomed to incredible proportions, teasing his waking mind and tormenting his sleep.

But Sam was not a fanciful man. The necessity to care for his family at an early age had aided in the development of a man who was down-to-earth, levelheaded and totally pragmatic. Logic told him that only in fairy tales did a noble but impoverished knight win the princess by slaying the fire-breathing dragon. A grim smile formed on his lips as he imagined Abby's probable response to that scenario. She'd undoubtedly insist on slaying her own dragon.

"Damn it, Garrett," he muttered, flinging himself into the leather chair behind his desk, "this is ridiculous. Get back to work."

He made a valiant effort, but her image appeared on every piece of paper, her throaty voice reverberated inside his head, and finally, giving in to impulse, he picked up the phone, dialing her number. When he got her answering machine, Sam crashed the receiver down and rose from behind the desk, pulling his jacket off the coatrack.

"I'll be out for the rest of the afternoon," he informed the woman seated at a desk outside his door. She only nodded, appearing pleased to see Sam Garrett leaving the office.

As Sam drove up to Malibu, he asked himself why he was doing this. Why he was setting himself up for failure. Sam had never really known failure, in his professional life, or his personal life. Even that little fiasco in the Caribbean had

resulted in the closing down of a major cocaine manufacturing lab, several indictments in the States and the confis-
cation of a record amount of the drug. He'd even received
a commendation by the president, which admittedly didn't
mean a great deal to him, but had made his mother cry.

In his twenties, he had been one of the FBI's brightest
young agents—no case was too dangerous, no cause too
futile. If his superiors had been asked to name one fault,
they might have suggested Sam Garrett had a tendency to
be a bit too rash, too zealous. By his thirties, he'd mel-
lowed a bit; his recklessness had been tamed, he tended toward solving crimes with analytical reasoning, only
resorting to dangerous tactics as a final solution. He was
admired and respected by his peers and superiors alike.

His personal life had mirrored his professional one. When
he was young, he had found women a delightful diversion
and might have been accused of overindulging from time
to time in the pleasure they offered. While he never had
women swooning at his feet, he'd never been forced to go
searching them out, either. They just always seemed to be
there, smiling, attractive, and oh, so very willing.

Over the years he'd learned to be more discriminating,
his choices in women reflecting more depth, more substance. He'd found it necessary to enjoy their conversation
in the morning, as much as he had their lovemaking the
night before. Still, he never lacked for companionship. Sam
knew that he could have picked up the telephone and called
any number of intelligent, attractive women who'd be more
than willing to share the evening with him. But he hadn't
done that, because every woman he'd ever known paled in
comparison to Abby Swan. While he knew that he had
nothing to offer her, that a life with Abby was impossible,
he found himself unable to stay away. He had to see her. One
more time.

It was a paradox, he considered, pulling off the road across from her beach house. Sam Garrett, accustomed only to success, was parked in the drizzling rain, waiting like a lovesick teenager for the one woman he could never have to return home.

He sat in the car for two hours, silently cursing whatever design engineer had decided to turn what had once been a comfortable car into something resembling a sardine can. His long legs never fit into automobiles these days, and the prolonged confinement, as well as the weather, was playing havoc with his thigh. Still, he had no intention of moving from this spot until he'd seen her, spoken with her. But as Abby's car pulled into her driveway, Sam realized he had no idea what he was going to say.

Abby's heart leapt into her throat at the sight of Sam's car parked along the roadway, but as he crossed the street she schooled her expression to one of polite interest. His limp was worse today, but he still looked wonderful.

"Sam," she managed to greet him casually, "what brings you out on a day like this?"

Her gray eyes were guarded and Sam knew he was not the only one afraid of being hurt. He was standing only a few inches from her but it seemed as though they were separated by a crevasse as deep and as wide as the Grand Canyon.

"I wanted to see you." His statement was far calmer than his mood. Sam wondered if she could see the galloping beat of his heart.

It took a major effort, but Abby kept her eyes level. "Oh? I suppose this is where I ask why."

Her expression was exasperatingly calm, but Sam heard the tinge of hurt mixed with accusation in her quiet tone. "Do you want the official reason?" he asked, his eyes capturing hers, holding her hostage to the turmoil building within him. "Or the truth?"

"Truth," she insisted softly.

They were standing beside her car, neither had made a move to go in out of the drizzle. Raindrops were scattered over her hair, appearing like diamonds on black satin. She'd pinned it back into a sophisticated twist Sam suspected had a name, but he had no idea what it might be. He knew only that he didn't like it; she looked too cool, too distant.

He reached out, plucking a pin from the ebony coil. Abby put a hand up to stop him, but when Sam shook his head in denial, she slowly lowered her hand to her side. He could feel the tension radiating from her as he continued to extract the hairpins, until her thick waves were falling over her shoulders.

"I couldn't stay away from you, Abby," he admitted, lacing his fingers through the silken strands. "I tried—God, how I tried—but I had to see you again." He tucked a strand of hair behind her ear as his eyes swept over her face. "Touch you again." He ran a finger down her cheek, feeling her involuntary tremor. "Kiss you again."

Abby watched, curious at the flare of anger blending uneasily with the desire in Sam's eyes. Then he was crushing her mouth in a swift, hard kiss that burned away all coherent thought.

He was almost savage in his need, taking what he wanted recklessly, ruthlessly, and although Abby realized through her spinning senses that she should be afraid of such raw power, she knew only a thrilling sense of inevitability. She had no thought of denying Sam anything, no wish for him to end this brutal kiss that was causing her blood to run hot with shared passion. She clung to him, aroused, enthralled, experiencing a kaleidoscope of blinding colors flashing behind her closed lids.

When his teeth bit lightly into her lower lip, Abby moaned; when her tongue darted into the dark interior of his mouth, in a feverish demand that equalled his, Sam shuddered, pulling her against him, lifting her hips into the thrusting strength of his loins.

"Yes," she murmured, dragging her lips from his to rain a blizzard of kisses over his face. "Oh, yes, Sam. Come inside with me. Now."

One moment Abby was discovering ecstasy in his arms, a second later she was released so suddenly she almost collapsed.

"Abby..." His eyes blazed with self-recrimination as he took in her full lower lip. Already the ripe pink was darkening and he knew he had bruised her tender skin. He'd never done that before, forced himself on a woman. What was the matter with him?

She reached up, pressing a finger against his lips. "Don't," she pleaded. "Don't apologize. And please, don't tell me you didn't mean it."

"I'm not going to tell you that, Abby. Because I did mean it. You know damn well that I want you," he said almost angrily.

She managed a soft smile, but there was no light in her eyes at his gruff confession. "I know."

"It's not a good idea," he continued harshly, trying to convince himself as well.

"Don't I get a vote?" she asked with outward calm. Inside her nerves were standing on edge.

His eyes raked over her. She'd lost even more weight since the day he'd foolishly called her to his office when a telephone call would have done the job as well. She'd misunderstood that invitation and he'd hurt her. Sam didn't want to do that again.

"I'm not like the men you're used to. I've almost been killed, I've spent half my life dealing with the type of scum that would make those bad guys on your celebrated television series look like Eagle Scouts. You need someone who'll treat you like you deserve, like fine porcelain." He shook his head. "I've forgotten how to be gentle, Abby, if I ever knew how to begin with."

Her eyes flashed with something amazingly like anger. "I'm not asking you to be gentle, Sam Garrett," she shot back. "I'm asking you to come inside and make love to me." She went up on her toes, her palms framing his face. "Please, Sam," she coaxed prettily, her eyes silver pools of need.

"Damn you, Abby," he swore softly, "this is unprofessional, crazy and downright dangerous."

"I know," she murmured, punctuating her words with kisses. "Let's be unprofessional, Sam." She pressed her lips to his. "Let's be crazy." Her tongue traced a tormenting trail from one side of his mouth to the other. "Let's live dangerously. Just for tonight."

Her soft lips, her liquid eyes, her caressing hands, all conspired to scorch the last remaining traces of sanity from Sam's brain. Muttering a short, harsh oath, he scooped Abby off her feet, flinging her over his shoulder.

"Sam!"

"I told you I wouldn't be gentle, Abby," he warned, ignoring the pain in his leg as he marched up her wooden steps.

"Is this the way you sweep a lady off her feet?"

"You want to be treated like a lady, go find one of your fancy Hollywood types," he growled, taking the key she dangled out to him and opening her door. Kicking it shut behind him, he climbed the stairs, dumping her unceremoniously onto the bed.

He stood over her, hands on his hips. "I'm through playing games," he informed her, his tone harsh and ragged.

Abby propped herself up on her elbows, the dark traces of desire in her eyes assuring him that whatever their differences, they were united in this overwhelming need for each other.

"It's about time," she said simply.

Sam told himself that of all the risky stunts he'd pulled in his lifetime, this one would have to take first prize. Unable to resist her silent lure, he sat down on the edge of the mattress, his fingers cupping her chin. When his thumb stroked her throat, he felt Abby's pulse quicken, but the beat was strong and sure.

Then he bent his head, losing the ability to concentrate as Abby met his lips with a devastating fervor.

11

SAM TRIED TO REMIND HIMSELF to be tender, to take his time, to savor this reunion. But passion set its own pace as Abby's hands roamed over his body in fitful desperation, her tongue probing, seeking, tasting of his mouth as if she were breaking a long fast.

The sound of the surf echoed the roaring in his ears as she fumbled with the buttons of his shirt, releasing one after another until she was finally able to press her palms against his bare chest. Sam shut his eyes at the fire her touch kindled in the pit of his stomach.

She had too many clothes on; he tore the belt away with impatient frustration and a moment later the white jacket was flung onto the floor, followed in short order by her silk blouse. His pulse leaped at the sight of the lacy chemise, her firm breasts rising and falling under the peach satin. *Slowly,* he warned himself, *the memory of tonight will have to last you the rest of your life.*

Abby was aware of the softening of his touch and although she wanted to cry out for Sam to take her now, she allowed him to set a more leisurely pace. Taking a deep breath, she tried to still her pounding heart, attempted to soothe the burning ache that spiraled outward from her very core. Sam was a frustratingly independent man. Abby knew that there were so many things that stood between them—her money, her name, her career. He'd never willingly accept anything from her. But she could give him this.

She forced herself to relax, to allow her limbs to grow heavy and weak as his dark gaze warmed her blood. She lay on her back, her eyes gilt silver invitations as she offered herself to him.

His fingers toyed with the ribbon straps of the chemise, slipping one off her right shoulder, pressing kisses along the warm skin, before repeating the gesture with the other ribbon. The chemise clung to her curves, exposing the ivory satin of her skin.

"I've been dreaming of this," he said, plucking at her lips as his hands traced the shape of her breasts. "I've been aching to touch you, taste you, learn what makes you moan with pleasure and cry out with passion."

His tongue left sparks as it glided down her throat, moving steadily lower, inch by glorious inch. "I've been going out of my mind remembering how that cool composure you show to the world is only an illusion to hide the uninhibited woman underneath."

His words echoed dully in her mind as Abby's body grew taut with need. "Please," she murmured, encouraging him to quench the fire whipping through her, "you haven't been the only one going crazy, Sam."

His eyes flamed at her admission. "Is this what you want, Abby?" he asked, his tongue circling one rigid, aching nipple.

"Oh, yes," she sighed, closing her eyes to the tantalizing torment.

"And this?" he murmured, plucking at the tender tip. "Do you like this?"

She was beyond words, instead she thrust her hands through his hair, pressing him into her yielding softness. Sam obliged, taking her nipple into his mouth, creating havoc with his tongue, his lips, his teeth, until Abby thought she'd explode. His hair brushed her flesh as he moved to the other breast, treating it to a drugging pleasure every bit as glorious.

She was liquid satin shimmering in his arms; while his mouth lingered at her breasts, one hand splayed across her abdomen and the other slid beneath her skirt, moving up her nylon-clad thigh to discover the soft mound between her legs. He pressed his palm against her, rewarded by her low, lingering moan.

His lips returned to cover hers and Abby was vaguely aware of Sam undressing her, of lifting her hips off the mattress as he slid the skirt and her panty hose down her legs. They had entered a realm where time no longer held meaning and every gesture, every lingering kiss could have lasted minutes, hours or an eternity. Soon she was lying naked in his arms, and as his hands and lips explored every gleaming inch of her, Abby had never been so aware of her own body.

Just when she'd decided she loved the feel of his wide strong palms stroking the bared flesh of her abdomen, Sam altered their position, and she wondered why she'd never known that her ankle was such an erogenous zone. She was melting, flowing under his touch, denying him nothing as Sam explored every inch of her.

When she felt the crisp hair of his chest brush against her back, she realized he'd undressed as well, but she had no idea how he'd managed the feat while never ceasing his arousing caresses. *Perhaps he's magic,* she considered dizzily, closing her eyes as his lips left a moist trail of fire down her spine. Only a sorcerer could create as much havoc with her senses as Sam was doing with his magical hands and mouth.

She cried out as his teeth nipped teasingly at the back of her knee and then she felt as if she were floating as he turned her in his arms once again.

"Look at me, Abby," he requested, his voice rough with barely restrained passion.

Slowly, as if coming out of a trance, Abby's eyelids fluttered open, her gaze colliding with his.

"Tonight you're mine, Abby."

He was braced over her, hard, lean, so blatantly masculine Abby thought she might die of the desire she felt for this man. She nodded, knowing that after tonight she would be Sam Garrett's woman forever; she could never belong to any other man.

"Tell me," he demanded roughly. "I need to hear the words."

Abby pressed her lips against his. "Yes," she whispered. "Yours, Sam. Only yours."

Unable to restrain from touching him any longer, she traced the curly mat of hair that bisected his chest, trailing her finger tips down the thick dark ribbon over his flat stomach. As her fingers moved ever lower, ultimately circling him, Sam groaned, thrusting his hips into her touch.

"I can't wait much longer," he warned, feeling the explosive warmth rising as Abby's slender hands stroked him with an instinctive sensuality that was driving him insane.

"Don't wait," she invited, guiding him to the welcoming warmth between her thighs. "I want you, Sam. Now."

He gripped her hips, seized by a blinding need for possession that surpassed anything he'd ever known. Abby gasped as he thrust into her, but then her long legs wrapped about him, and she repeated his name, over and over again, in a litany of love as the final flash consumed them both.

"Oh, Abby," Sam said with a sigh, after a long, silent interval.

Abby had been lying beside him, her head on his chest, feeling drowsily content. Now she risked a glance upward, viewing the pain in his eyes. Still luxuriating in the pleasure she'd experienced in Sam's arms, it was almost too much to bear. How could she feel so blissful, when he was obviously suffering so?

She pressed a quick, hard kiss against his lips, forestalling any further words. "Don't be sorry, Sam," she said quietly. "I'm not. What we just shared was wonderful. Please don't spoil it by apologizing."

"I should be sorry," he said, "but I'm not. I've wanted you from the beginning, Abby."

Her hands trembled only slightly as she cupped his face in her palms. "And I've wanted you," she admitted softly. "I love you, Sam. I'll always love you." There, she'd said it and she was glad it was finally out in the open.

He shook his head, dragging his gaze from her wide, luminous eyes to stare up at the ceiling. Abby's heart was in her throat as she awaited his response. "Don't," he said finally. "Don't love me, Abby. I'll only end up hurting you and that's the one thing I never wanted to do."

A terrible tension filled the air, swirling about them, and Abby shivered slightly, dreading what was coming next. Feeling her slight tremor, Sam reached down and pulled the sheet up, covering them with a field of yellow daisies.

"I've been offered a promotion," he said bleakly, still not looking at her. "In Washington." There were hard lines around his mouth, and Abby closed her eyes against the inevitability of his next words. "I'm thinking seriously of taking it."

A dark, cold wave swept over her, like the vicious riptides in the seemingly placid waters outside the window, threatening to drown her. Abby fought against it, refusing to allow anything to spoil their magical time together.

"I see," she said with outward calm. "Congratulations."

She touched his shoulder, but Sam pulled away from her. Her heart went out to him as he stood and walked to the window. His back was stiff, but she could detect the limp she knew he was trying to hide. He kept so much from her, she thought. Abby couldn't believe that Sam didn't love her. She'd seen it in his eyes too many times. The problem, she decided sadly, was that Sam didn't want to love her. She began to shiver with the horrible fear that he was actually strong enough to deny that love.

"How can you say that?" he asked quietly, almost viciously. "If you really loved me, how could you be pleased about this?"

She couldn't miss the skepticism in his tone and her hands nervously smoothed out the wrinkles in the sheet. "I want you to be happy," she answered simply. "If this promotion means that much to you, I'd never think of asking you to stay here." *With me*, she added silently.

He spun around, his hands curled into fists at his hips. The despair in his eyes slashed at her heart like a rusty knife. "I don't give a damn about the promotion," he said roughly. "But don't you see? I have to get away. I can't stay here, wanting you, knowing that I could never have you."

"I love you," she said simply.

He stared at her for a long moment, wondering how he could ever make her understand. If Abby did love him, and he had no reason to doubt her softly stated words, how could he make her understand that sometimes love wasn't enough?

"It would never work." His voice was hoarse. "Love is a pretty word, Abby, but it can't survive without respect."

"I respect you." How could she not? Sam was the most decent, honorable man she'd ever met. In fact, Abby considered, if he wasn't, this scene wouldn't be taking place.

"I couldn't respect myself," he said harshly, brokenly. "Not while I was living on my wife's money."

"If that's our only problem, Sam," she argued, "we'll live on yours."

His eyes roamed the room, settling on Abby's clothing scattered across the floor. "Do you really believe I could afford the little niceties you've always taken for granted?" he asked caustically. "That little silk suit probably cost more than a month's pay. Come on, Abby, do you know what a government employee makes? Do you have any idea how the real world lives?"

Abby wasn't going to give up this easily. "I have all the silk suits I need," she replied calmly.

"Damn it, can't you understand? Even if you could get used to living on an FBI agent's salary, you have your career to think of. You can't run around Hollywood looking like Little Orphan Annie." His lips twisted into a tight grimace. "I've lived here long enough to know that image is everything. You said that yourself when you didn't want to take my car to the bank. It didn't live up to your image, Abby. *I* wouldn't live up to your image."

His tone cut deeply and she was out of the bed like a shot, glaring up at him. "How can you think I'm that shallow?" she retorted.

His eyes narrowed. "Are you telling me you'd be happy living in some little tract house instead of this place?" His hand swept the room, including the panorama outside her window. He pinned her with an intimidating gaze Abby secretly decided must work very well when he was interrogating suspects.

"Do you expect me to believe you'd rather stay home, ironing my shirts and baking apple pies, than having all those people at your beck and call at the studio?"

Realizing that this might well be the most important conversation she'd ever had in her life, Abby forced herself to tell the truth.

"If you were the richest man in the world, I'd still want to work, Sam. It took me a very long time to escape from under my father's thumb and gain my self-esteem; I couldn't give it up." Her soft eyes pleaded with him to understand. "Not even for you."

"And there'd be no ego-gratification in being Mrs. Sam Garrett, is that what you're saying?" he asked grimly.

If that was a proposal, Abby considered, it was the vaguest one she'd ever heard. It crossed her mind that she could simply drop this argument for the time being, agree to whatever Sam wanted, and work on changing his mind after he'd married her. But they were both incredibly strong-willed individuals. There would be enough adjustments to make without starting things out on a lie.

"Nothing would make me happier than being your wife," she said truthfully.

"Why do I hear a *but* in that little declaration?"

She put her hand on his arm. "Because I need my work, too. Would you be happy staying home all day and puttering around some workshop in the garage?"

"It's different and you damn well know it," he countered.

"Why are you allowed to be more than husband, but I'm supposed to view myself only as a wife?"

"Because I'm a man, dammit!" he roared.

Abby didn't believe Sam was as chauvinistic as he was sounding. There had to be more and she thought she knew what it was. "What if I wanted a more conventional career? Like an attorney? Or a banker, or computer programmer?"

He shrugged. "That wouldn't bother me," he admitted.

"So, you're leaving me because the great Sam Garrett's ego can't handle being married to an actress, is that it?"

"Not just an actress," he pointed out grimly. "You're a star, Abby. I doubt if there's anywhere in the western world you could go without people recognizing you. You're a household name." He shook his head with honest regret. "I couldn't handle being Mr. Abby Swan. I couldn't face myself in the mirror every morning when I shaved, knowing everyone thought I was living on my wife's income."

"You could always grow a beard," she suggested with a soft, encouraging smile, her fingertip stroking his harshly set jaw.

"This isn't anything to joke about," he stated flatly.

Abby read the finality in his eyes and sighed. "No, I can see it isn't," she agreed quietly. "So, you're really leaving."

"Yes." The single word did not come easily to him.

"When?"

"As soon as possible. Within the week."

Abby bit her bottom lip to stifle her cry at the pain his words instilled. "Then this is all we're going to have."

He had never experienced such agony as that brought about by Abby's quiet, accepting tone. "It's more than I should have allowed," he replied soberly.

She managed a wobbly smile and her arms went up to circle his neck. "Well then," she said a little breathlessly, "let's not waste any more time arguing. Please, darling, let's make the most of this night."

Her arms tightened and Sam's answering embrace crushed her against him, so tightly that for a moment Abby found breathing an impossibility. Still she clung to him, exalting in his strength, vowing to put everything out of her mind except the sheer glory of this man's body pressing against hers.

"God, Abby," he groaned into her hair, "what am I going to do without you?"

"No," she insisted. "Don't think about tomorrow, Sam. There's only now. Only the magic of this one perfect night together."

Her mouth clung to his, smothering words Sam knew should be said. But the friction of her body against his drove all thoughts of resistance from his mind. Desire was white hot, as her desperate passion inflamed him and all he could think about was making love to her again. And again.

He dragged her to the floor, his lips moving feverishly over her body. As he took her in a wild blaze of passion, Abby wept silently, unaware of the tears streaming down her cheeks.

Abby had no idea how many times she and Sam had turned to each other during the night, but each time their lovemaking had been more intense, more desperate, as if their passion could keep the sun from rising. Finally, exhausted, they fell asleep in each other's arms, succumbing to the inevitable.

SAM WOKE FIRST, his mind instantly alert. Abby was curled against him, her head resting on his chest. A pearly pink glow filtered in the window, signaling the rising dawn as it cast shimmering lights on her dark hair. Her lips were parted slightly as she slept, the sheet had fallen away and as he watched her breasts rising and falling, Sam was struck once again by her fragility. Even before her obvious weight loss, she'd been smaller than her screen image; he knew his fingers could span the delicate bones of her wrist with room to spare.

Her complexion was flushed a deep rosy tone, her long lashes a thick black fringe against her cheeks. She appeared so warm, so desirable, so infinitely tempting. And vulnerable, he reminded himself with a stab of guilt, trying to fight his renewed hunger as she shifted in his arms, fitting her slender frame against his body.

Unable to resist, he bent his head, pressing a light kiss against her sleep-tousled black hair. A smile touched her lips and for a moment he was afraid he'd awakened her. But she expelled a soft sigh and her eyes remained closed, allowing him the unadulterated pleasure of watching her without fear of detection.

He wondered why he'd never noticed that slight tilt to her nose before and decided that when Abby's lustrous gray eyes were open, they eclipsed her other features.

That he wanted her again came as no real surprise. He always wanted her. Last night he'd been like a starving man presented with a sumptuous banquet. He'd tasted of her again and again, but had not been able to satiate his overpowering hunger. Now, in the pearly shadows of morning, he wanted nothing more than to stay here, keeping her beside him, sensuously, gloriously naked. It was more than the mere need to possess her; what he felt for Abby Swan was no less than obsession.

Unable to remain in bed another minute without making love to her, Sam slid from her light embrace, retrieving his clothing from the floor. He stood in the doorway, giving her one long, last look, before heaving a deep sigh and leaving the room.

ABBY'S FIRST THOUGHT as she began to awaken was that she was unusually stiff this morning. Her limbs ached, and her entire body felt abnormally heavy. Then, gradually, she remembered, and a warmth infused her, banishing the lingering achiness. Sam. Wonderful, sexy Sam. She rolled over to take him in her arms and found sheets that were cold in the damp morning air.

Pain twisted her heart, then spread its dark and evil force through her body, infiltrating her every pore, gripping at her stomach like an enormous fist. She was out of bed, running down the stairs, mindless of her undressed state.

"Sam!" She rushed into the kitchen, experiencing a rush of joy so strong she thought she might faint.

He turned, tensing immediately as he viewed the terror in her eyes. His hands curved over her shoulders, finding her flesh icy cold. "Are you all right?" he asked quickly. "Did something happen?" He hadn't been able to stop worrying about her, despite the fact that the majority of individuals working on Abby's case had all but closed the file. It had all been too easy. Too pat.

She rested her forehead against his shoulder, expelling a soft sigh. "Oh, Sam," she whispered. "I thought you'd gone."

He put his arms around her, his palms moving in comforting circles against her back. "I wouldn't leave without telling you goodbye, Abby," he said roughly.

She wrapped her arms about his waist, leaning against him. Sam could feel the wild beat of her heart against his chest. He pressed his lips again and again over her tousled black hair, murmuring low, inarticulate words of comfort.

He'd meant to soothe her, but his words, his touch, everything conspired to rekindle Abby's desire. "Come back to bed with me, Sam."

He brushed her hair away from her face, looping it behind her ears, framing her uptilted face with his hands. She was so lovely, so inviting. There was nothing he wanted more than to spend the rest of his life making love to Abby Swan. But that was an impossible wish and to give in to her softly issued request would only postpone the inevitable, only make their parting that more painful.

"Abby..." He shook his head regretfully, telling himself that a clean, quick break was the only way.

Her eyes were eloquent in their need. "I've never begged for anything before, Sam," she confessed quietly. "But if that's what it takes to lie in your arms one last time, I'll do it."

"God, Abby," he groaned, realizing how it must feel to keep sinking deeper and deeper into quicksand. "I don't want you to do that. Don't you know that leaving here is going to be the hardest thing I've ever done?"

Abby was tempted to ask him not to leave, to stay here with her forever. Whatever problems they had, they could work out together. But she read the terrible finality in his eyes and knew that Sam had given the matter serious consideration and had made up his mind.

"Then make love to me," she said. "We'll forget who we are, what brought us together, and what's keeping us apart. I'm simply Abby and you're Sam, and we only want a few fleeting hours of shared pleasure before our lives take us in different directions." Her words were tinged with a touch of desperation as her hands encircled his neck. "If this is all we're going to have, let's at least allow ourselves this one final memory."

His eyes softened as they roamed the delicate planes of her face, drinking in her features, knowing the memory of loving Abby would stay with him always. He lowered his head, covering her lips with his, kissing her with a gentleness he would have thought himself incapable of a month ago. He'd always considered himself a nice enough man, an adequate and considerate lover.

But none of the women he'd ever known in the past were anything like Abby. While she'd possessed the ability to drive him up a wall with her periodic stubbornness, her inner softheartedness brought out a tenderness he hadn't known he possessed. She was like silk—so soft and feminine on the outside, but possessing the tensile strength of steel.

"Abby, are you sure?" he asked, the hand that stroked her face none too steady.

Her eyes gave him her answer first, glowing with a warm light of love. "Yes, Sam," she whispered. "Yes. I'm very sure," she said, as she began to unbutton his shirt.

He couldn't think when she touched him. Her fingers were like a flaming brand, and Sam scooped her into his arms, holding her against his chest as he climbed the stairs to the bedroom. He'd allow himself this final pleasure, praying that it would be enough to last him the rest of his life.

THEY WERE LYING in each other's arms, neither one ready to shatter the beauty of their time together with the words that must be spoken. Sam had come to the realization that a life without Abby was simply not a life worth living. But what could he offer her? Then the idea that had been teasing at the back of his mind suddenly came to him, with such a blinding, startling clarity Sam was stunned he hadn't figured it out before.

"I've got to go," he said suddenly.

Abby's arms tightened around him. "Not just yet."

He kissed her gently, and the smile on his face was not feigned. "I'll be back," he promised.

Her eyes held little seeds of doubt. "Promise?"

"Promise. What are your plans for today?"

"I told Ken I'd go sailing with him, but I can always cancel."

He shook his head. "There's no need to do that. What about this evening? Any plans?"

"No," she said hesitantly, afraid to hope for too much.

Sam grinned. "Good." His gaze shifted to her closet. "Do you have something in there suitable for celebrating?"

"Celebrating?" A puzzled little frown drew a line between her brows and he reached out a gentle finger, brushing it away.

"Celebrating," he confirmed. "Because when I come back tonight, I'm taking you for a night on the town. Dinner, dancing, the sky's the limit, sweetheart."

She shook her head. Now that she'd been open with Sam, she didn't want to deceive him. "I'm trying to be a good sport about all this, but I don't think I can celebrate your promotion, Sam," she whispered sadly. "Not when it means I'll never see you again."

He planted a quick, hard kiss against her lips. "That's not what we're celebrating."

She watched him picking up the scattered articles of clothing from the floor. "Then what?"

"Trust me," he invited, pulling on a pair of briefs.

"I do." Her luminous eyes echoed the softly spoken statement.

He dressed in a hurry, gave her one last breathtaking kiss, and then, smiling back at her, left the room. Abby heard him taking the stairs two at a time and wondered what on earth had gotten into the man.

Then she smiled to herself as she remembered the past several hours. She wasn't going to dwell on the negative. Sam was coming back. He'd promised. And although it might only be for tonight, at this point, Abby was only going to think about one glorious, love filled night at a time.

The smile was still on her face as she showered, dressed and drove down to the marina to meet Ken.

12

THE RED SAILS of the *Black Swan* whipped in the breeze as Abby and Ken skimmed along the top of the water, headed up the California coast. The seas had been calm when they'd started out, but now the water was becoming more and more choppy as the skies darkened and the winds picked up considerably.

"Ken, don't you think we should head back?" Abby asked. She was not nearly as skilled a sailor as her brother.

He gave her a teasing grin. "Frightened, Abby?"

"Not really," she hedged, unwilling to admit she was more than a little uneasy. "I know you're an expert sailor, but everyone else went in an hour ago."

"I prefer a challenge. There's nothing like beating the odds, wouldn't you say?"

"There's also nothing like staying alive," she retorted, as she was suddenly drenched by a high, forceful wave. "Damn it, Ken, I want to go back!"

She had no idea of the time, but they'd been out here for most of the afternoon, and if she was going to wash the salt from her hair and get ready for Sam's surprise, Abby wanted sufficient time to prepare. For personal reasons, she wanted to be at her most glamorous this evening.

"We can't always get everything we want, kiddo," Ken said casually, altering their course, taking them farther and farther out to sea.

"Ken!" Abby yelled over the wind and crashing waves. "I want to go home this minute!" If she'd been standing up, she would have stomped her foot.

"Sorry. I can't do that."

"Why not? Just turn the boat around and take us back to the marina," she insisted.

Ken appeared not to have heard her. "You know, life is funny sometimes," he stated conversationally.

Abby was drenched as yet another wave washed over her. "This is no time for a philosophy lecture."

He continued to ignore her. "Like the way I was Matthew Swan's firstborn, not to mention his only son, but you ended up with all the marbles." He shook his head. "Ironic, isn't it?"

He had to shout to be heard over the wind and water, but Abby couldn't miss the note of icy anger in his voice. "I've done my best to make that up to you," she protested.

"Yes, little sister, I'll give you that. But no matter how much I do, you're still the one with controlling interest. And after your birthday, you'll have absolute control. You'll still hold the purse strings. Every cent goes straight to you, and if you get tired of me, you can cut me out, the same way our father did."

"I'd never do that," she objected.

When he failed to answer, Abby's eyes darted about, seeing nothing but dark, storm-tossed waters. This was incredibly foolhardy, she told herself. And dangerous. Another idea came to the forefront of her mind, but was so horrible that she didn't want to believe herself capable of such a thought.

She leaned forward, putting her hand on his arm. "Ken, let's go back to the marina and we'll talk about this."

He shook her off, his eyes glittering as they raked her face. "It's too late, Abby. It's a shame, really, that things have to end this way. You see, I'd been planning something a little different for you, but your boyfriend managed to find that guy who wrote you the first note, so it was back to the old drawing board." His cold smile sent a chill racing up Abby's spine. "Fortunately, I am an inventive man."

Abby stared at him. "You sent those other letters, didn't you? And sabotaged my air gauges. And turned on that burner."

"Of course. It was actually very easy. I bought the paper and mailed the letters on my trips out of town. The scuba diving accident looked like a sure bet, but then you changed your plans and went down with those other divers who proved an irritating nuisance. I thought the burner was inspired, especially with *People* magazine so helpfully letting everyone know about your bedtime tea habit."

He shook his head, eyeing her with undisguised malice. "Who would have thought you'd be diligent enough to go out and buy a smoke detector? I'll say this for you, little sister, you've been a continual source of surprises.

"The light was a little tricky, but—" he shrugged "—where there's a *will*, there's a way." He smiled at his double entendre, but there was no warmth in his expression.

Abby's blood had turned to ice. "Sam was right. Someone was trying to kill me. *You* were trying to kill me."

"Sam was a pain in the neck," he ground out. "It was such a carefully thought out plan; then he had to go and ruin it."

"You were going to kill me, then let an innocent man go to prison?"

"Innocent?" He stood up, causing the sailboat to tilt precariously. "What about me, Abby? Wasn't I innocent? Did I deserve to be disinherited for my parents' sins?"

Abby put her hand out, schooling her voice to a calm, collected, reassuring tone. "Ken, please sit down. You're going to capsize us."

He did as she asked, but his eyes took on a strange, remote look that did nothing to soothe her ragged-edged nerves. "You're going to have another accident, Abby. And this time, I'm afraid it's going to be a fatal one."

He picked up a large wrench from under a tarp, and as he headed toward her, Abby knew, without a single doubt, that Ken had every intention of killing her, here and now. She wasn't strong enough to fight him off; her only hope was escape. Jumping up, she closed her eyes and dove into the water, gasping as the cold shocked her system.

Then, her arms beating furiously against the strong waves, she headed toward shore, glancing back in time to see Ken waving the weapon over his head in a burst of frustrated rage. His attention on Abby, Ken didn't see the enormous wave headed toward the *Black Swan*. Moments later the boat was capsized, but Abby didn't wait for Ken to surface. She kept swimming, telling herself over and over she had to get back to shore. To Sam.

SAM WAS WHISTLING as he entered the federal building. Things were definitely looking up. His appointment had gone as well as he'd hoped, what he'd shared with Abby last night had left him bathed in a glow of well-being, and tonight he was going to bridge the gap between Abby and himself once and for all. Things couldn't be better.

His secretary looked up at his approach, her face set in an earnest expression. "Mr. Garrett, Paul Fletcher is in your office. He says it's urgent."

Sam's stride quickened as he nodded and moved past her desk. Paul Fletcher had been analyzing Abby's letters. Now what?

"We got the handwriting analysis done," the blond-haired man stated without preamble the moment Sam walked through the door. "The last seven letters were written by someone different. It's a careful forgery, but not good enough."

Sam felt his heart stop. "Got a line on the author?"

The agent's face was grim. "It's the brother. When this thing first started, we took a sample of everyone's writing, just as a matter of course. The guy did his best to change everything, but there's enough conformity to stand up in court."

Sam uttered a short, harsh oath, pulling his gun from a desk drawer. "Call the Malibu police and the coast guard," he instructed tersely, leaving the office on a run. "Abby's out sailing with the guy right now. Have them meet me at the marina."

THE POLICE HELICOPTER had been circling the area for the past fifteen minutes while Sam kept the binoculars glued to the waters, searching for the crimson sails of the *Black Swan*. He'd told Abby that he'd never shot anyone in the line of duty, but if Kenneth Swan succeeded in his plan, Sam knew himself capable of killing the man.

"It's damn rough down there," the pilot offered. "A small craft could capsize real easy. If she's in the water, she's going to have a hard time of it."

"All the more reason to find her as soon as possible," he muttered.

"Hey, we're trying."

"Trying's not good enough, dammit!"

Sam was suffused with a sense of his own inadequacy and guilt as his careful gaze swept over the harsh sea, looking for some sign of Abby or the sailboat. He couldn't imagine a life without Abby. He had to find her, had to make things work. If anything happened to her . . .

"Hey, what's that?" The pilot's voice broke into Sam's tortured thoughts.

"Where?"

"Three o'clock," the pilot said, pointing. "I just saw something moving."

"Probably a damn dolphin," Sam muttered, not wanting to allow himself any false hopes. He moved the binoculars in the direction indicated by the pilot, his eyes narrowing as he tried to focus on the dark object bobbing in the waves.

"It's her!"

"I'll call the coast guard and give them her location," the pilot offered, reaching for the radio.

"It'll take too long," Sam objected. "We'll have to bring her up."

"In this wind? Hell, even if you could get a line out to her, it'll be miracle if we can pull her out of there."

"It's my day for miracles. Let's go," Sam instructed, getting up to retrieve the life ring.

At first Abby thought she was imagining the noise throbbing in her ears, but as the wind began to whip the water about her with increased strength, she glanced upward, her heart leaping as she viewed the police helicopter. She tried to wave, but the movement only caused her to go under, where she was tossed violently, her lungs feeling like they were going to explode.

Sam watched, his heart in his throat, saying any number of silent prayers. When her head finally reappeared, he felt like cheering.

"We can't go down any lower," the pilot said, "or we'll make it even harder on her. This baby creates one helluva draft."

Sam pushed against the force of the air, opening the passenger door. He tossed the ring in Abby's direction, but it fell short, bouncing ineffectively in the whitecapped waves.

Growling a short expletive, he hauled it in, the second try ending up far to Abby's right. "Third time's the charm," he muttered, flinging it once again to within a few feet of where she was making a valiant attempt to tread water.

As the heavy white ring hit nearby, Abby reached out, her leaden arms barely able to hold on. She was scared, frozen, and exhausted, but she'd come too close to death to allow fatigue to overcome her now. She clung to the life ring with all her strength, willing herself not to give up.

A moment later, an orange canvas sling hit the water beside the ring, and although it took some careful maneuvering, she held herself afloat as she climbed into it. Curling her frozen fingers about the rope, she closed her eyes, and prayed that she wouldn't discover a fear of heights.

The pilot worked to hold the craft as steady as possible in the winds buffeting them as Sam slowly, steadily pulled Abby out of the water.

"That's it, babe," he murmured encouragement Abby had no way of hearing. "Hold on, we're almost there."

A sudden gust of wind caused the helicopter to suddenly tilt and the canvas sling to sway wildly several feet over the water. Sam muttered something that was part oath, part invocation as one of Abby's hands tore loose. A moment later she had things under control and he began to breath again.

Abby's scream had been whipped away by the wind as she'd almost fallen back into the black, swirling waters, but she forced herself not to become hysterical as she gripped the ropes with renewed strength, resting her head against them. She kept her eyes closed, but she could tell by the increased draft, and the loud sound from the helicopter rotors that she was drawing steadily nearer to safety.

Just when she thought she couldn't hang on a moment longer, she was swept into a pair of strong arms.

"Sam! You came!"

"Of course," he said simply, his matter-of-fact attitude belying the terror he'd been feeling for the past excruciatingly long minutes. "I told you once, Abby, you're stuck with me. For the duration."

She reached up, pressing her hand against his cheek, needing to reassure herself that Sam was real, and not just some hallucination. "I'm glad," she whispered. "So very glad."

"Hmph." The pilot self-consciously cleared his throat. "I hate to interrupt, but we need to get the lady back to medical care as soon as possible."

"Of course," Sam said instantly, pushing Abby gently into a seat and buckling her in. He took the one beside her, wrapping her in a blanket and enclosing both her chilled hands in his.

"Do you happen to know where the sailboat is, Ms Swan?" the pilot asked. "If I could give the coast guard a ball-park fix, it'd help us find it. And your brother."

"To hell with that guy," Sam returned harshly. "Just get us back."

Abby's face displayed her inner pain at Ken's betrayal. "It got capsized by a wave," she explained, "right after I dove into the water. I don't know how long I've been swimming, but since I drifted a bit, I'd say it's probably somewhere back there." She pointed toward the southwest.

"That's close enough," the pilot said, radioing in the *Black Swan*'s possible position as he turned the helicopter back to the marina.

Moments later they'd landed and a crew of paramedics wrapped Abby in dry blankets and set to work checking her pulse rate and blood pressure. They had an ambulance waiting, they assured the visibly anxious man hovering over her.

"I don't want to go to the hospital," Abby complained.

"You've suffered a shock, Abby," Sam explained. "You need professional care."

"I need care, all right," she admitted, "but not the kind I can get in a hospital. I want to go home."

"I don't know," he said, wanting nothing more than to be alone with Abby, but not wanting to endanger her further.

"She'll be okay, so long as she stays in bed and keeps warm," the paramedic suggested.

"That's precisely what I had in mind," Abby said, her eyes gleaming invitations as she gazed up at Sam.

He raked his fingers through his hair, uncomfortable with his inability to make a rational decision. "I don't know, honey, perhaps we ought to at least have you checked out in the emergency room."

Abby rose, holding the blanket around her body in an amazingly regal gesture for someone who'd been through what she had recently suffered. "I'm going home," she announced, looking back over her shoulder. "Are you taking me, or do I have to hitchhike?"

"Stubborn," Sam muttered to one of the grinning paramedics. "This woman's going to drive me crazy."

"I can't think of any better way to go," the younger man offered.

"Amen, brother," Sam said, scooping Abby up to carry her to his car. "Amen."

Despite her allegations that she felt fine, once she'd had a warm bath, changed into a long flannel nightgown and allowed Sam to put her to bed, Abby fell instantly asleep. The room was dark when she finally woke.

"Sam?" Her eyes scanned the shadows, searching for him, a little part of her mind still afraid she'd dreamed the entire thing.

"Right here," he said, rising from a chair in the corner of the room and coming over to her. The mattress sagged as he sat down on the bed next to her.

"How are you feeling?" he asked, brushing back a few strands of hair from her forehead.

"I don't think I'll ever be able to move my arms again," she groaned. "And my legs ache something awful."

"You were swimming in some pretty rough waters. For a while there, I didn't know if we were going to find you. Did you say you dived out of the boat?"

Her eyes shadowed with a sudden pain. "I didn't have any choice. Ken—" Her voice broke.

"They found him," Sam offered, not particularly thrilled himself with the turn of events, but knowing Abby would be concerned.

"Is he . . . ?" She couldn't bring herself to say the word.

"He's alive," Sam answered brusquely.

Abby exhaled a sigh of relief. "I'm glad." Then her expression grew thoughtful. "I'll have to call Jordan first thing in the morning."

"Jordan?" Sam had an idea where Abby's train of thought was going and wasn't surprised. Neither was he pleased.

"He'll be able to recommend a good criminal attorney."

"You're going to pay for the guy's defense?"

"I don't think Ken really meant to do it, Sam," she protested softly. "He had a lot of understandable resentment in him that was misdirected. I still think we can work things out."

"He's going to have to go to prison, Abby," Sam felt obliged to point out. "Even a miracle-worker wouldn't be able to get him off scot-free."

She nodded. "I know. But I want him to have the best chance for rehabilitation. I really believe he's a good man, deep down inside."

"You definitely have a Pollyanna viewpoint on life, sweetheart," he accused. "You could probably find something of value in Jack the Ripper."

She grinned. "Now you're exaggerating. Besides, if I gave up easily on people I love, I'd have given up on you long ago, Sam Garrett. You were a tough nut to crack, you know."

He took her hand, bringing it to his lips. "I didn't want to get involved with you unless I could give you something of value," he protested.

Her eyes met his over their linked fingertips. "You're valuable, Sam. All by yourself."

"I wanted to do better."

Abby sighed, her fatigue returning as she realized they were about to rehash the argument over the disparity in their bank balances. Sam's next words came as a surprise.

"And I think I found something," he revealed, his gold eyes sparkling with devilish amusement.

"What?"

He gave her a broad, self-satisfied grin. "How would you like twenty million dollars?" he asked casually.

Abby's eyes widened, and she sat up in bed. "You're kidding!"

Sam looked as if he'd just swallowed the proverbial canary, cage, feathers and all. "Nope."

"What did you do? Rob a bank?"

"You're having lunch tomorrow with Torr Janzen."

"Torr Janzen! He didn't want anything to do with *Medicine Woman*!"

"He hadn't read it," Sam revealed. "Now he has, and he's falling over himself to package the deal. In fact—" he grinned wickedly "—if you don't hold out for one helluva percentage, I'm going to be disappointed in your business sense."

"I don't understand. How do you know Torr Janzen?"

"Remember about ten years ago, when Janzen's kid disappeared?"

"Vaguely. I was in college, so I didn't follow it as closely as I might have," she admitted.

He crossed his arms over his chest. "Well, you're looking at the guy who caught the kidnappers and returned little Lars safe and sound to his daddy, who was understandably grateful. Janzen told me that if he could ever do anything for me, all I'd have to do was ask."

Abby shook her head stubbornly. "So you asked him to back your lover's film. No, Sam. I won't use those tactics any more than I'll use Swan Pharmaceuticals' money," she stated firmly.

Sam reminded himself that Abby had been through a lot today. It was only the memory of her in those icy waters that kept him from losing his patience.

"You've got it all wrong. All I asked him to do was read the screenplay. He made the decision on his own, Abby."

"Really?" Her eyes were still skeptical.

Sam expelled a harsh breath of air. "Do you think the guy's stupid enough to bankroll a flop, no matter how he felt about keeping his word?"

Abby's fingers gathered the flowered comforter into folds as she considered Sam's statement. "No," she said finally. "I don't think so."

When she lifted her gaze to his, her eyes were suspiciously moist. "What can I ever do to thank you?" she whispered. "You've saved my life. Twice. You've gotten me something I was driving myself crazy trying to achieve. . . . I owe you so much, Sam. I'll never be able to pay back my debt to you."

"Oh, I don't know," he stated slowly, rubbing his chin. "We could probably come up with something."

Abby couldn't miss his sensual tone. "If we worked at it," she agreed breathlessly.

The smile that had been hovering at the corners of his lips suddenly vanished. His eyes gleamed, but once again Abby viewed that odd little shadow that had always hinted of a secret vulnerability in this strong, self-assured man.

"Marry me, Abby."

As much as she longed to shout out a loud "yes," there were still one or two points Abby needed to clear up.

"Marry?" she asked softly. "What type of convenient deal are you offering, Sam? And what happens when the balance of power shifts?"

He groaned. "I was afraid I was going to have to eat those words." He leaned forward, bracing himself with a hand on either side of her body as his face came within inches of hers.

"I'll admit I had a pretty bad view of marriage, Abby. But that's all changed because of you. How I feel about you."

"How do you feel about me, Sam?"

He shook his head, giving her a slight grin that Abby felt was directed inward. "You aren't going to make this easy on me, are you?"

She pressed a tender, lingering kiss against his lips. "It's just one little word. Would you choke on it, Sam?"

"Look, Abby, when I was in college, I thought I knew what the word meant. When my marriage failed, I decided it was only a fanciful illusion created by romance novels and schmaltzy movies."

Her palms framed his face. "And now?"

Sam closed his eyes momentarily, and Abby's heart went out to him. She knew that she was going to marry Sam, whether he told her he loved her or not, because she knew he did. Deep down.

"I love you, Abby," he said with a sudden burst of words. "I was going crazy out there when I thought I'd lost you. All I could think about was that I loved you so damn much I didn't know what I'd do if we didn't find you in time. If you wouldn't agree to spend the rest of your life with me!"

"And let you think I'm marrying you for that twenty million dollars?" she argued. "I loved you before you came up with that money, Sam Garrett. It's important that you realize that."

"All right, maybe I was wrong," he admitted.

"Not maybe. You *were* wrong."

"Abby," Sam groaned, "are you going to give me your answer or not?"

Her eyes sparkled as she chewed thoughtfully on a peach-tinted fingernail. "I'm thinking about it."

"Let me give you something to think about," he suggested, beginning to unbutton the flower-sprigged flannel nightgown.

"Sam," Abby protested weakly, as his fingertips brushed sparks against her skin, "you're distracting me."

"That's the plan," he murmured, cupping her breasts with his palms.

"What about my work?" she managed to ask with a thin thread of sound. "I love you, Sam. But I don't want to give it up."

As he met her wary gaze, Sam realized how hard it had been for Abby to be honest about her feelings. She deserved the same from him.

"I won't say it'll be easy," he admitted. "But I figure if you can put up with all my bad habits, I can live with the fact that my lady is both talented and rich."

"It's probably a good thing I am," she suggested. "Since commuter marriages aren't cheap."

"True," Sam agreed. "But that's a moot point; I'm not going to Washington."

"But your promotion," Abby objected. "I don't want to stand in the way of your career, Sam."

He pressed a quick kiss against her lips. "You're not," he assured her. "I never wanted to take that job; I'd go crazy locked up in headquarters, spending all my time behind a desk. At least here I'll be able to take part in the less vigorous fieldwork from time to time."

"Nothing dangerous," she said sternly.

Sam grinned down at her. "Nothing dangerous," he agreed. "I promise to stick to things like rescuing beautiful damsels in distress."

"You go rescuing any other women, Sam Garrett, and you'll discover it's a lot more dangerous than tracking down drug dealers." The sparkle in her eyes belied her censorious tone.

Sam gave her a salute. "Yes, ma'am."

Abby sighed happily. She was definitely the luckiest woman in the world. "I love you, Sam."

"And I love you, sweetheart," he murmured as his lips followed the trail his hands had blazed down her body. Not only had it been much easier this time, Sam was surprised at how good it felt to say those words aloud.

"By the way," he tacked on casually, "after your lunch with Janzen tomorrow, we're flying down to Mexico."

"Mexico?"

"How does La Paz sound for a honeymoon?"

Her fingers twisted in his chestnut hair as Abby yanked his head up.

"Ow!"

"Pretty presumptuous, aren't you?" she asked, her eyes shining.

"Always," Sam agreed. "Any objections?"

Abby laughed. "You're in luck, Sam Garrett, FBI," she said, punctuating her answer with stinging little kisses against his smiling mouth as she began undressing him. "As it happens, La Paz is my second favorite place in the whole world." She tossed his shirt onto the floor and her fingers moved to his belt.

"What's your first?" he managed to ask, as his slacks joined the crisp dress shirt.

Abby's eyes gleamed a dazzling silver as she provocatively lifted the corner of the sheet.

"Guess."

Sam needed no further invitation. "In that case," he said, a slow smile creeping across his face, "perhaps we should just spend the rest of our lives right here."

As he drew her into his arms, Abby could not think of one single objection.

Harlequin Temptation

COMING NEXT MONTH

Take 4 books & a surprise gift FREE

SPECIAL LIMITED-TIME OFFER

Mail to **Harlequin Reader Service®**

In the U.S.
901 Fuhrmann Blvd.
P.O. Box 1394
Buffalo, N.Y. 14240-1394

In Canada
P.O. Box 2800, Station "A"
5170 Yonge Street
Willowdale, Ontario M2N 6J3

YES! Please send me 4 free Harlequin Superromance® novels and my free surprise gift. Then send me 4 brand-new novels every month as they come off the presses. Bill me at the low price of $2.50 each—a 10% saving off the retail price. There are no shipping, handling or other hidden costs. There is no minimum number of books I must purchase. I can always return a shipment and cancel at any time. Even if I never buy another book from Harlequin, the 4 free novels and the surprise gift are mine to keep forever.

134-BPS-BP6S

Name _____ (PLEASE PRINT)

Address _____ Apt. No. _____

City _____ State/Prov. _____ Zip/Postal Code _____

This offer is limited to one order per household and not valid to present subscribers. Price is subject to change.

DOSR-SUB-1R